ABIGAIL TO THE RESCUE

I heard a gunshot crack. And another. Horses thundered into camp. I dropped my tools and dashed out of the tunnel.

A blur of mounted Indians whirled and whooped near the cabin. Dick crouched in front of it, rifle shouldered, and fired. Garrett's Dragoon boomed from his position, which was stock-center in the canyon. His target catapulted backward off his horse.

Flaming torches arced through the air, landing atop the cabin. A screaming brave swinging a stone-headed club heeled his horse straight at Dick. I whirled to get my Sharps from the shaft.

Hunkering behind a slag heap, I sighted a painted chest and fired. He jerked upright, then pitched from his mount.

Dick lay crumpled beside the campfire. Behind him, thick smoke boiled from the burning cabin. Garrett pivoted, slapping his pistol with his palm, but it was jammed. He dropped to his knees and sprawled in the dirt.

I fired . . .

REDEMPTION TRAIL

The spirited and exciting adventure of one unforgettable frontier woman— and the true grit that helped her win the West.

FROM SPUR AWARD-WINNING
WESTERN WRITER

SUZANN LEDBETTER

TRINITY STRIKE

From the heart of Ireland comes the irrepressible Megan O'Malley, whose own spirit mirrors that of the untamed frontier. With nothing to her name but fierce determination, Megan defies convention and sets out to strike it rich, taking any job—from elevator operator to camp cook—to get out west and become a prospector. In a few short months, she has her very own stake in the Trinity mine— and the attention of more than a few gun-slinging bandits. But shrewd, unscrupulous enemies are lurking, waiting to steal her land—and any kind of courtship must wait. . . .

from Signet

Prices slightly higher in Canada.   (0-451-18644-3—$5.50)

Suzann Ledbetter

REDEMPTION TRAIL

A SIGNET BOOK

SIGNET
Published by the Penguin Group
Penguin Books USA Inc., 375 Hudson Street,
New York, New York 10014, U.S.A.
Penguin Books Ltd, 27 Wrights Lane,
London W8 5TZ, England
Penguin Books Australia Ltd, Ringwood,
Victoria, Australia
Penguin Books Canada Ltd, 10 Alcorn Avenue,
Toronto, Ontario, Canada M4V 3B2
Penguin Books (N.Z.) Ltd, 182–190 Wairau Road,
Auckland 10, New Zealand

Penguin Books Ltd, Registered Offices:
Harmondsworth, Middlesex, England

First published by Signet, an imprint of Dutton Signet,
a division of Penguin Books USA Inc.

First Printing, April, 1996
10 9 8 7 6 5 4 3 2 1

Prelude

Abigail groaned some as she slowly raised the lid to the wooded chest. The box exhaled the scent of lavender sachets, cornstarched linens, and aging notepaper intermingled with the sweetly cloying aroma of cedar, which always brought the memory of a long-ago rainy June morning to her mind.

A small, leather-bound journal lay atop a mound of tissue-wrapped, bygone finery. Abigail placed the book in her lap, caressing its water-marked, grainy surface. Its string-stitched binding creaked, much like her knobbed knuckles, as she gently turned back the cover.

The inscription on the flyleaf brought a pensive smile. "Gracious, how strong and curvaceous my script was forty years ago," she murmured. "No sign at all of the jagged, staggering scratches that now ramble from my pen."

Abigail closed her eyes to the wan sunlight

braving the attic windows' dusty panes. In an instant, she felt transformed. Gone was the life-weary crone who spent too many days impatient for pain-free, peaceful eternity to just damn well get on with it. For a moment, she was that copper-haired, devil-take-it twenty-year-old with a head full of golden dreams and a future as infinite as the Rocky Mountains' spiked backbone.

"Ah, yes, the good old days," Abigail said with a chuckle. She licked a fingertip and leafed to the diary's first entry.

"I didn't know it then, but those months in Colorado were the most exciting, heartbreaking, wondrous times of my life."

April. Wednesday, 10th, 1861

Snowed all night and still snowing now,
but I started for Denver City, wind right
in my face and the snow blinds me. Almost
hard to keep road at all. I got down to
Steels Hotel and there I stopped. Could
not go any further. Snowed all day,
snow in places is two feet deep, six inches
on level.

I awakened with my belly rumbling like an ore wagon. When I'd blown in the night before with a blizzard at my back and not a nickel to my name, the hotel's wizened desk clerk had taken pity on me. The storeroom's cot proved a rickety affair, but its blankets smelled of lye soap and sunshine. I slept as cozy as a cradled infant.

The ecstasy of stretching sore limbs into usefulness brought vapors puffing forth like a fairy-tale dragon girding for battle. Drafts seeped through hasty chinks, stirring scents of lemon rind, onions, and salt meat.

Hunger gnawed on my backbone. I recalled Sunday's greasy, spit-cooked rabbit and a half-frozen biscuit: a meager repast, and a fatal one for my beloved father. That Maximilian Roswell Tremain Fiske choked to death on a sliver of lodged bone was too ironic for a playwright's plot.

"You were a dashing dreamer, a drunk, and a conniver, Papa," I whispered to the log walls. "And the best, most loving father a motherless little girl could hope to have."

Night after night, posturing on the tailgate of our garishly painted wagon, Dr. Maximilian R. T. Fiske cured me of a horrendous palsy with a scant teaspoon of his eighty-proof Miracle Nerve & Brain Elixir.

The bottle used for demonstration purposes contained nothing more than molasses and honey thinned with tea: a palatable concoction, but one I grew to detest the taste of.

Papa's secret recipe for the salable variety, which he mixed in an iron cauldron as needed, relied heavily on grain alcohol. It not only "suspended" the baking soda, sugar, cinnamon, hops, gunpowder, and cayenne he added with a heavy hand, his tonic would resist freezing even during the coldest winter nights and surely took the chill off its users as well.

"I ask you, ladies and gents," he'd inquire in a stentorian tone, "is there the slightest tremble now afflicting this poor waif?"

Papa'd lay his hand on my shoulder and lower his voice. "Come closer. Examine carefully the steadiness of her hands. How her unsightly facial tics have vanished, instantly, with only one infusion of Miracle Nerve and Brain Elixir.

"But, you say, what can it do for me who, praise the Lord, does not suffer from a debilitating palsy like this unfortunate girl?

"Friends, this tonic's curative and preventative properties vanquish poisons in the blood, nervous diseases, dyspepsia, weak digestive organs, piles, cankers, night sweats, kidney complaints, catarrh, and biliousness.

"It breaks my heart to tell you, folks, if only I'd known how a Nebraska minister's wife suffered from female complaints, her husband would be alive today. Driven to insanity by the miseries of her gender and with no Miracle Nerve and Brain Elixir to provide relief, she murdered her dearly beloved in his sleep."

With that anecdote rattling in their minds, astounded audiences all but stampeded to buy Papa's gilt-embossed pint bottles for a mere dollar each.

When circumstances called for an alternative profession, Papa, the Reverend M. R. T. Fiske, restored my sight, my hearing, or straightened my twisted clubfoot, fervently assuring the multitudes that such Divine Intervention would be visited upon all true—and generously tithing—believers.

And though the clouds rarely cooperated, famous meteorologist Professor M. R. Tremain Fiske, Esquire, soaked every drought-stricken community in Iowa for the services of his roaring, guaranteed-within-two-weeks rain-making machine.

The cot wobbled and creaked as I hugged myself tightly, trying to banish the bittersweet memories. Tears rose and spilled over.

"Colorado was to be our Promised Land, Papa," I whispered. "Our golden opportunity to settle and be respectable. A hundred times, I could've lost you to a bullet or the noose, only for you to strangle on your damned dinner."

I swiped my streaming face with the scratchy covers and threw them aside. Cringing when my socked feet met the cold floorboards, I snatched the hand-me-down, four-buckle gaiters from beneath the cot frame.

"He called me tougher'n post oak, smarter by half than most men he ever knew. Guess the time's come to prove it."

From my pack, I tugged out a high-collared, gunmetal gray suit—the kind one buys for its durability, later praying for a tragedy like a stoveblack stain so it can be scrapped for rug braids.

Slipping the voluminous creation over my cotton scout shirt and denims, I vowed to torch the godly frock at the first opportunity and never repeat the error.

The fabric was as creased as a farmer's brow, but the worst offenders smoothed out with the flat of my hand. I pretended the scuffed, stubby-toed boots peeking beyond the hem were black kid oxfords with ribbon laces.

Careful not to let the screen door slam behind me, I departed through the trade entrance as the desk clerk had advised and hastened around the building to the street.

I startled at the movement of what I thought were bundled rags stuffed in a packing case. A gurgling cough echoed from within as a filthy moccasin emerged with bare toes wriggling out the split seam.

Hundreds of destitute emigrants rambled the city's treeless streets trying to survive the winter months on scraps, handouts, and hope. It frightened me to admit the only thing separating me from them was a nameless hotel clerk's compassion.

It seemed every member of Denver City's colorful, varied, and somewhat soap-temperate population chose this morning to brave the elements. Miners, merchants, buffalo-robed Indians, gamblers, and silk-hatted lawyers jostled their way past. None were old; in fact, few had reached middle-life. I appeared to be the only one wearing a chemise beneath my shirt.

I asked a Bible-clutching parson for directions to the El Dorado Parlor-Saloon. His bulbous nose wrinkled as if a foul odor had invaded it. He pointed westward and failed to bid me a good day.

By its posh name, I expected to find a smoke-hazy gentleman's club with a potted fern or two, brass cuspidors, and a number of antlered trophies peering blindly from their mahogany mountings.

Instead, the foyer's pink, flocked wallpaper partially corrected my presumption. A life-sized portrait of a reposed, bovine brunette wearing nothing but a string of pearls, several strategically placed feathers, and an un-Christian leer banished it completely.

Motion on the stairway caught my eye. A Negro boy tiptoed down the creaky runners like a burglar. "Can I do ya fer somethin', ma'am?"

"Is there a Garrett Collingsworth on the premises?"

He chewed a knuckle thoughtfully. "Uh, no, ma'am. He done come in a while's back and done gone inta the parlor over yonder."

I thanked him and whisked through the portiered doorway he'd indicated. The room's roughly ten-by-ten dimensions contained enough furniture and bric-a-brac for three its size, which gave it all the gentility of a train wreck. Amid the jumble, a great bear of a man sat at a table reading a newspaper.

Quietly slipping out of my pack and mackinaw, I laid them and my rifle on an ugly horsehair settee. A hammering heart made an aura of supreme confidence all the more difficult to achieve.

"Excuse me, sir, I'm Abigail Fiske. I believe you're expecting me?"

Dusky, long-lashed eyes glanced up, over his shoulder, and back again. "I'm waiting for a man by that name—"

"My father was called to Glory on Sunday instant, Mr. Collingsworth. It's left to me to tend his share of the prospecting partnership."

He nodded, gesturing toward an adjacent chair. Rather than object to his obvious assessment of my charms as I sat down, I returned the scrutiny in kind.

The jut of his ears held back waves of shoulder-length dark hair, framing a neatly trimmed beard and mustache. He was twenty-five if he was a day, twenty-seven at most. Although his hands bore the scars and calluses of a common laborer, his fingernails were clean as a banker's.

"I feel kind of cheated by destiny, Miss Fiske. From our correspondence, I looked forward to meeting your father. I'm real sorry I'll not be getting the chance."

My chin trembled and I stiffened, fighting for composure. On the mantel, a Waterbury's pendulum switched as loud as a ball peen on tin. "I may be a poor second to the arrangement, but have no doubt that I'll earn my share of its bounty."

His brows collided above the bridge of his nose. "There's no earning to be done, ma'am. Mr. Fiske wired his hundred-dollar grubstake weeks ago. You have my word that a quarter of any gold we find is yours."

"Such trust will come easy since I'll be there helping divide the spoils."

"What do you mean, *be* there?"

"At the diggings, of course." Steel edged my voice, though he didn't seem particularly cowed by it. "As I said, I fully intend to fulfill Papa's share of the bargain."

Collingsworth shook his head. "No way, nohow, little lady. I admire your gumption, but a miners' camp's no fit place for a woman."

"Oh, bullfeathers."

"Miss Fiske—"

"Abigail's my given name. I'll thank you to use it." Planting a forearm on the table, I leaned toward him like a guard dog on a short lead. "Gender has nothing to do with the business at hand, Mr. Collingsworth. I can work as hard as any man, draw down on our supper, skin it, and cook it.

"I've ledgered accounts since the age of six, drove a team at eight, have more medical know-how than a lot of sawbones with shingles swinging from their awnings, and as Papa'd tell you if he were here, I don't need anyone to take care of me, tell me what to do, or how to do it."

The prospector's cheeks flushed as rosy as Rome apples. He reached for his coffee cup and took a long pull at the contents.

I clenched my fists so tightly the knuckles blanched. In my mind, I heard Papa cluck his tongue and say, *Confrontation only heightens a disagreement; it rarely lessens one. Finesse, Abigail. Will you ever learn the fine art of finesse?*

Collingsworth cleared his throat. "There's probably lots of men in Denver City that'll appreciate those talents." Chair legs puckered the flowered rug as he scooted back from the table. "Unfortunately, I'm not one of them."

He stood at least six-foot-four, shoulders wide

as an ox yoke. Looking up at his rock-solid frame, I felt the same sense of abandonment I had when Papa breathed his last.

"Forgive me, please, for my rudeness," I said softly.

Hazel eyes pegged my brown ones. "No need for that. A gal's gotta have sand to get by in these parts. Never have understood how the meek propose to inherit the earth or how they'll manage if they do."

"Then why are you so angry with me?"

A smile widened the part in his mustache. "I'm not angry. We just don't have anything else to talk about and there's chores to do before we leave out tomorrow."

"What time shall I be ready?"

Instantly, his expression rivaled a hanging judge's. "You're not going, Miss Fiske. Raise all the hell you want, but that's the way of it." He took a step toward the door.

I leaped after him, tugging at his sleeve. "No, I'll tell *you* the way of it. If I'm not fit for this expedition, Papa's money isn't, either. I demand its return."

"It's already spent for provisions and supplies. I doubt if me and the boys could raise six bits between us."

The emotional toll of the last two days squeezed my heart like a cider press, I bowed my head, speaking more to myself than the man staring at me irritably.

"I don't have anywhere else to go; no money to stay here. Being Maximilian Fiske's daughter is all I know how to do . . . and I guess I'm not really that, anymore."

All that'd kept me going since I buried my father in a half-caved, shallow mine shaft was fulfilling his dream—a last, grand adventure, he called it. We'd sold everything to meet that hundred-dollar stake, with just enough left over to keep body and soul together for the long march from Topeka.

Nobody knew us in Colorado. Hard times and all those warrants, with Papa's name misspelled but the charges clear as branch water, that had haunted us the last few years were supposed to disappear at the borderline.

A rough finger slid beneath my chin. Collingsworth raised my eyes to his, obviously searching for a trace of guile.

"Traipsing about with the likes of me, Ransom Halsey, and Dick Curtis'll ruin your good name, Abigail."

"Why? Because I choose to work for my keep rather than beg for it? I don't need your protection. I need a partner, and maybe a friend."

A heavy sigh brushed my face. By the vein

pulsing at his temple, conscience must be waging a silent war with good judgment.

"I reckon Lillith can put you up here for the night," he said. "We'll light out at midday, but I'll caution you here and now: Pull your weight and hold that temper or I'll send you packing."

My spirits soared; I could have helped roosters rouse the town, and curled my toes inside my boots to stifle the urge. "Bless you, Mr. Collingsworth."

"Garrett's my given name and I'll thank you to use it." A lopsided grin belied his mockery. "And I don't know what you're blessing me for unless it's for plumb taking leave of my senses."

April. Thursday, 11th, 1861

Busy all morning getting ready to start.
Got a good dinner and then started out. Got
about eight miles up Cherry Creek and
then camped. Weather cool and cloudy.

Playing possum, an art I practiced to perfection
from the tender age of five, educated me in ways
that would have prematurely whitened my father's hair had he known how raptly I absorbed
every word of his and his friends' midnight stag
sessions.

Among other things, the existence of and en-
tertainments available at a bordello were hardly
unknown to me, though I'd never participated in
such procreational contortions and, frankly,
didn't believe some I'd heard described were possible, let alone desirable.

Despite my uncustomary worldliness, dis-
covering that Lillith was Garrett Collingsworth's

older sister, the El Dorado Parlor-Saloon's madam, and the creature portrayed so flagrantly in its foyer rendered me speechless.

Jezra, the Negro houseboy, relayed those facts yesterday afternoon while showing me to my quarters. Upstairs, soiled doves varying in age, nationality, attractiveness, and states of undress pointed and giggled from their rooms as we strode by.

According to my escort, the El Dorado was the most exclusive sporting house in Denver City. It maintained that title by only opening its doors to guests between the hours of four o'clock in the afternoon and two o'clock in the morning, unless Lillith agreed to make special arrangements in advance.

Motioning me into a sumptuously appointed boudoir, Jezra said, "The mens'll be arrivin' directly. Bolt up behind me and don't peek your nose out 'fore daylight 'lest you see flames lickin' the rafters. Don't want them fellers thinkin' you're a sweetheart."

"That could be an embarrassment to all concerned," I agreed.

"Yes'm, and Miss Lillith ain't partial to ruckuses. If'n you need anything, give that bell cord over yonder a smart pull. I'll scat up here, soon as I can."

"Whose room is this, Jezra? I've never seen such finery."

"Miss Lillith's. With Master Abercrombie stayin' down to the Jefferson Hotel, she won't be needin' it this evenin', nohow."

The next morning, as I was sipping strong black coffee from the stove's graniteware pot and found myself alone with my musings, I gazed at the early sun spilling weakly onto the bordello kitchen's shellacked floorboards. On the window-sill, a water-filled Fleur De Lis Bust Creme jar held geranium sprigs reaching bravely toward the frosty glass.

I turned at a rustling sound, like dry oak leaves crackling underfoot. Had I not recognized her from the painting, I'd have guessed the regal, elegantly attired woman standing in the doorway and holding her hands for mine to clasp had once trod the halls of Windsor Castle.

Hugging me to her ample bosom, Lillith Collingsworth kissed my cheek, then stepped back to view me from widow's peak to trouser rolls.

"Last time I saw you, you were wearing a polka-dot pinafore with a dribble of strawberry preserves down the skirt."

As I could manage nothing but stunned stammerings, she explained, "Maximilian and I met fifteen years ago in Omaha. I remember him fretting so for your future; that he would fail as father as he had as a husband. I knew otherwise, and you've become a lovely young woman, which proves his unwavering affection. And my good judgment."

My eyes stung with tears I'd held back too long. Lillith rocked me side to side as I sobbed all over her aqua silk wrapper. Such maternal comfort made me feel small enough for pinafores and pigtails again, and I was profoundly grateful for it.

"Better now?" she crooned. "A good cry cleanses the soul without dulling the memory."

Looking into her brilliant green eyes, I knew I was in the presence of a good woman, regardless of her occupation. I would not ask, nor did I care whether she'd known Papa in the biblical sense. In fact, I hoped they had found solace in each other's company.

"How can I ever repay you for your hospitality and kindness, Miss Lillith?"

"Give them to another needful of it and share tales of your adventures with me when you return."

She gathered up my belongings from the floor and steered me toward the foyer. "My brother's waiting for you at the mercantile. He's not renowned for patience."

"From our talk yesterday, I'd say there's a passel of stubborn mixed in, as well."

"Don't let Garrett bully you. He's a fine man, but, alas, a man all the same. In His infinite wisdom, God didn't provide us with alternatives."

Outside, slushy snow drifted against the storefronts, which made each step an awkward trial. My rubber-soled boots held out the moisture, but cold seeped in like smoke through gauze. Typical of boomtowns platted at sunrise on butcher paper with lots sold and temporary lath-and-stretched canvas structures erected by nightfall, Denver City's streets narrowed, widened, bent, and crossed as if a stray dog had guided their construction.

As quickly as the nearby foothills could be stripped naked of trees, sturdier structures replaced the founders' flimsy originals, but their awnings jutted out or cowered like little boys called to the front of the schoolroom for a recitation.

PIKE'S PEAK BOOT & SHOE EMPORIUM. HOSTETLER'S DRY GOODS. PHINEAS T. EYMOR, DRUGGIST.

I scanned the various white-lettered proclamations shouting from their lofty, false-fronted heights and wondered who inspired the notion to slap two-storied facades on single-storied buildings, and what earthly purpose such ramparts were supposed to serve.

Blake Street's screechy, gambling-hall orchestras competed at putting passerbys' teeth on edge. Those who'd never heard a piccolo, cornet, fiddle, and wheezy piano in concert could not appreciate the horrors of their combination.

I spied Garrett and another man cinching a tarpaulin over an enormous, speckled mule's laden back. The animal seemed determined to uphold its forebears' ill-natured reputation by stamping globs of soupy clay mud all over the cursing packers.

"Damn you, Stoophy," Garrett's assistant bellowed. "Stand still or I'll cosh ya betwixt the eyes and sell ya for horsemeat."

"Good morning, gentlemen," I greeted them cheerfully.

Both glared at me as if I'd insulted their sainted mothers, so I mutely watched a caravan of freighters churn sloughs in the boggy boulevard.

Presently, Garrett saw fit to introduce me to Stoophy's owner, Dick Curtis. His sunken eyes and cheeks bespoke consumption, but the wiry, camber-backed Forty-Niner appeared as nimble as a cougar.

"Can ye cook?" he asked around a stogie clamped in the corner of his mouth.

"Passably fair," I answered. "Can you?"

"Hmmph. 'Bout the same. That yer pa's Sharps?"

I glanced at the rifle canted against the hitch rail. "My father couldn't hit a locomotive at ten paces. If we had meat on the table, it was me that put it there."

"That so, eh?" The cigar wobbled and rolled over. "Ever kilt a man?"

Risking a sly wink, I replied, "Not yet."

One eye squinted against the curling smoke, drawing Dick's homely face into a comical leer. "I reckon I'd best mention that I've lasted two score and six without no skirt giving me what for. I'm a blasphemin', whiskey-swiggin', soap-hatin' son-of-a-soldier and I'll be one 'til I get planted."

I stuck out a mittened hand and grinned. "Just stay downwind while you teach me this romantic business of mining and we'll get along fine."

We shook on it, then Dick and Garrett ambled inside the mercantile to pick up the last of the supplies, leaving me in charge of Stoophy and her anonymous, drowsy companion.

"Sumbitchin' tinhorn!" boomed a passing bull-whacker. "Clar the road afore I plow ya under!"

An impossibly handsome young man was mired squarely in the path of a thrashing ox team. Arms bent at the elbows, knees pumping like twin pistons, his forward progress could have been measured in inches.

The bullwhacker reared up. His rawhide whip slithered on air, its crack as smart as a rifle shot. Goggle-eyed and straining, the oxen swerved around the terrified pedestrian.

"Oughta lay that lash to you whilst I'm at it," the driver snarled.

A spot of clay smirched the ambulator's cheek-bone like a birthmark. Fair-haired, sky-eyed, and clean-shaven—a rarity in this frostbiting climate—he smiled at me, revealing pearly whites as even as fence pickets.

"Are you all right, mister?" I inquired.

"I'd rather you hadn't witnessed my come-uppance, Abigail, but I appreciate your concern."

If employed to deliver *Hamlet*'s stanzas, his sultry baritone would surely cause many a Ladies' Theatrical Arts Society to flutter their fans with vigor.

"How do you know my name?"

He chuckled and doffed his splattered derby. "Stoophy gave a better clue than Garrett's description, I assure you. I'm Ransom Halsey, fourth swabby on this overland voyage."

I felt a flush rise up my neck at the thought of being rendered less recognizable than a stupid mule. "And how, may I ask, did Garrett describe me?"

"As I recall, he said you were about twenty, a spinster, rather tall, and more railed than rounded."

"Oh, he did, did he?" A fair tempest brewed in my head. Spinster, huh? And a skinny one at that. Had the lumbering lout been standing there, I swear I'd have kicked his shin.

"Ah, here comes the other half of Collingsworth and Company," Ransom said. "Garrett, Dick, I feared you'd been set upon by cutthroats."

"If you'd moseyed over in time to help load, we'd be a couple miles outta town by now," Dick growled.

He and Garrett bucked heavy cloth sacks of flour, beans, and cornmeal onto the pack tree strapped on the second mule's back. Smaller pokes of sugar, salt, rice, coffee, and other digestibles chinked the gaps, with my possibles and Ransom's tossed atop the pyramid.

"Now make yourself useful and snug down that canvas, Halsey," Dick ordered. "And none of them granny knots, you hear?"

With Garrett in the lead, Dick tugging Stoophy's harness, Ransom following with Remus, the second mule, and me trailing at drag, we departed Denver City. Yet, its silhouette hardly shrank into the horizon before we stopped at Carruther's Ranch for dinner.

Other than the thick slabs of beefsteak draping the rims of our plates, the establishment's moniker had no connection to cattle raising.

"In Jefferson Territory, a ranch is more likely a lodging house than a cow-calf operation," Ransom explained. "Don't know the why of it, just happened that way."

I devoured the fried meat, fried potatoes, fried cornmeal mush, and fried apples heaped in front of me, stealing peeks at my oddly assorted partners.

For a lanky gent, Dick shoveled food down his gullet like a squirrel sensing a hard winter ahead. Staring blindly at the room's hewn log walls, Garrett seemed completely lost in thought, taking no notice of what his fork deposited between his teeth.

Ransom attempted to converse with each, to no avail.

I, too, would have welcomed a friendly repartee, but like the two other male statues sharing the table, the blonde gladiator who'd flirted with me a few hours earlier now acted as though I were invisible.

Maybe if I learned to spit, scratch what itched, and curse more eloquently, I'd be treated less like a tag-along child. Not that I wanted to make a spectacle of myself, but on no less authority than Papa's discerning eye, and regardless of

Garrett's appraisal, I'd been told that my thick, coppery hair, porcelain complexion, and comely contours often induced corn-fed dowagers to grip their suitors' arms more tightly when I passed.

But if the stone silence, interrupted only by smacking lips and utensils scraping against tinware, was any measure of my feminine wiles or our company's camaraderie, the next quarter year promised to be the longest of my life.

The door banged open. Snow swirled around a filthy, hulking nightmare of a man. The shaggy hellhound at his side appeared almost as dangerous as his master. One staggered, the other slunk to a far table, their combined stench as horrific as a sun-bloated corpse.

I must have gasped aloud, for Garrett leaned toward me and said behind his hand, "That's Phil the Cannibal—it's wise to pay him no mind. They say he's wanted back East for murder. Brags he gobbled a couple of Indians and a Frenchman one winter when he ran out of grub."

My own lunch commenced a Virginia reel. The vile creature hunkered over his plate, stuffing meat and bread in his mouth with grimy fingers. It was the most revolting human display I'd ever witnessed. I couldn't take my eyes off him.

"Can't imagine it myself," Dick said, "but Big

Phil swears that the head, hands, and feet, when cooked through, taste like pork. Rest of us ain't much of a meal. Too gristly and tough."

The chair shot from behind me like a cannon-ball. I stomped outside, pulling the door shut so vigorously that icicles fell from the eaves like crystal daggers.

I tried convincing myself that the men were just bedeviling me. When they emerged a few minutes later as somber as pallbearers, a shudder raced through my body from hairline to toenails.

Silly goose, I chastised myself. Ghouls don't roam free in the United States of America or her territories. Yet, I'll admit, I checked our back trail regularly for several days.

Angling southeastward, we met up with and paralleled Cherry Creek's meandering bank. For two, maybe three miles, whomperjawed tents, crude shacks, and the frozen carcasses of pack animals rested among the chokecherries the creek was named after.

From an Indian encampment, a rank odor, like burning rope, wafted toward us. Knowing it was rude if not life-endangering to stare boldly at the natives, I ducked my chin and aimed shrewd sideward glances.

Other than their painted, skin-stretched shelters and animal-pelt garments, the tribe performed daily chores not unlike we pale-complected villagers would. The women were doing most of the work; the men stood or squatted, discussing Lord knows what, and the children played and romped among themselves.

An odd-looking object hissed and popped in the middle of the communal cookfire. A more brazen inspection showed it to be a large dog, staked upright on stubbed legs and roasting merrily—hair, hide, tail, and all.

Papa'd mentioned once that some tribes paid town boys a bounty to scavenge gutters for dead dogs. To their palates, roast cur was a delicacy and not a bit went to waste.

At that moment, I wished I hadn't listened so closely to my father's anecdotes, or at least that my memory of them was more faulty.

What manner of place was this Colorado, where dogs and their masters could be hunted down as dinner rather than hunting together for it?

To take my mind off such gruesome subjects and because I'd also become quite familiar with the rhythmic sway of Remus's plump hindquarters, I gandered at the Rockies' sawtoothed, snow-blanketed peaks.

Towering pine trees and firs terraced up the forbidding slopes like theatergoers standing for an ovation. Higher up, the mountains' jagged, forbidding features were left exposed by swirling, sweeping winds.

Mile after sloggy mile, I hiked in Remus's wake, my boots rising and falling more from habit than from conscious thought.

Despite the scenery's savage beauty and my delight at glimpsing a mule-deer doe and her fawn bounding gracefully through the forest, lawsy, my thighs and calves ached like fire. The Sharps I cradled seemed to gain a pound every half hour.

Surely we'd come far enough to cross the Mexican border at any moment.

Naturally, I lied a blue streak when Garrett hollered over his shoulder, "Hey, Abigail. Getting tired?"

Staggering out from behind Remus, I answered, "Tired of watching this mule's tail twitch."

"How about you, Ransom? You're looking a tad saggy in the knees."

"I'm fine . . . for another mile . . . or two."

"Good enough. Night slams down fast in this country. We'll set camp first level place we find."

Hearing Ransom mutter "Praise the Lord and hallelujah," I whispered a heartfelt "Amen," refusing to anticipate what new tortures might lie ahead.

April. Sunday, 28th, 1861

Took out about $2.50. Ground frozen.
Had a good time with boys. Weather
pleasant.

Seventeen days ago, when our company left
Denver City, I didn't know we were aiming for
no particular destination. Without the mountains indicating which way was west, the only
directions I could have pointed to now, with any
assurance of accuracy, were up and down.

We'd crossed several slushy creeks, and some
kindhearted pioneer had graciously spanned a
sizable river with a lashed log bridge. Though it
was reputed to be healthful, I'd found the crisp
mountain air more like beggar's porridge: too
thin to be satisfying.

The men complained of aches, lighthead-
edness, and frozen toes. As the lone representative of the weaker sex, I felt duty-bound to

merely plod along and save wind. I couldn't fathom why, but my dependable good cheer seem to irritate my companions somewhat.

When en route to Denver City, Papa and I'd whiled away many an hour discussing the wondrous luxuries we'd partake of when the Mother Lode presented herself, but he'd wasted few words explaining how one went about making her acquaintance.

I'd presumed clusters of gold would show themselves on the ground, sort of like bear scat. Along the untold miles we'd roamed, not a pine needle nor a pebble escaped my scrutiny, which testified to my diligence; and, I soon learned, my ignorance.

For the umpteenth time, Garrett dropped to his knees beside a stream, yanked a grass clump from the muck, and stirred the roots in his gold pan. Except this morning, instead of cursing the day he was born and striking out again, he sat back on his heels and brayed like Stoophy.

"Show me for a fool or prove me right, Dick," he called, grinning broad as a boy.

The Forty-Niner tamped a finger in the pan-liquor, examined the tip as if he'd never seen it before, then commenced to rub it against his teeth.

Ransom and I glanced at each other. He

looked as dumbfounded by our partners' obvious mental derangement as I was.

Dick let out a war whoop worthy of a Comanche, his boots scattering pebbles in a crazed do-si-do. "Bless my soul and bury me deep! Them flakes is smoother'n a baby's butt. It's gold, children. No damned doubt about it."

I rushed over and gazed upon the precious speckles, no larger than sugar grains. The reason for Garrett's odd riverside rituals became clear. The tiny particles, dislodged and carried along by the water from their mountaintop lair, snagged in grass roots along the bank like blackberry seeds in a sieve.

A warm rush spread over me. Sweat popped out on my forehead. If Garrett and Dick were insane, it was a contagious affliction and I'd caught a bad case of it in the span of a clock's tick: gold fever.

Garrett insisted we set camp before robbing the stream of its plunder. He'd seen too many argonauts labor to exhaustion and nigh starvation when that Lorelei metal romanced their good sense. True enough, I trembled so from excitement that I could hardly drive my tent stakes into the frozen ground.

Dick, as cruel a man as our burly leader, proceeded to build a fire and prepare the midday meal. He assigned me the chore of scooping clean snow into a bag of flour and kneading it into dough. It was sheer misery suspending that lumpy mass, impaled on a forked stick, above the flames for what seemed like a month before it baked through.

Ransom, however, was given the more humbling duty of digging the latrine ditch, an enterprise Garrett praised him for becoming so accomplished at performing.

"By God, I ought to be good at it. I've tilled enough of them the last couple of weeks. Can't we just take our leave behind a tree?"

"Not all of us can," Garrett replied evenly.

After choking down victuals none of us held any appetite for, we set to the task of becoming fabulously wealthy. Garrett and Ransom trekked downstream a quarter mile, while Dick and I sunk to our ankles in silt a few yards from camp.

Sunlight glanced off my shiny, untried gold pan, shaped much like a giant's pie tin, its wide mouth and sides sharply angling to a bottom slightly larger than a saucer.

"Cant the lip away from you and dredge in a goodly dollop of sediment," Dick instructed, his actions matching his words. "Hold her steady and level in one hand, kindee flittering the other through the mud so the river'll sluice out the sand."

"But won't the gold wash out, too?"

He graced me with a Job-like smile. "Reckon if it did, I wouldn't tell you to do it that way, now, would I?"

I stuck my tongue out at the old rascal, then returned my attention to his gnarled hands, which were quickly taking on a bluish tint from the stream's icy baptism.

"Gold's heavier'n sand, gal. That's why it sinks to the bottom. All right, after playing pattycakes awhile, you spins and shakes it 'round this-a-way and that-a-way to rinse out more gravel. Then tip it a mite and go frontwards and backwards, letting the pebbles lop over the edge.

"Reel it outta the water, swirl it, then rinse the grit away, over'n over 'til there's nothing showing but a half-moon of black sand in the flange and heavier stuff in the crease."

I leaned closer, peering intently at the table-spoons of flotsam banked at the bottom. "Is that gold?" I asked breathlessly.

"Keep your knickers hitched, missy," he drawled. "We ain't near done yet."

The image I'd envisioned of a trove heaped taller than my tent by nightfall faded somewhat. Dick proceeded to add a scant bit of water to the remainder, smack the pan's edge with his palm, and swirl it clockwise.

Like magic, worthless dregs collected at the right side. On the left, trace glitter winked from the dark sand. My pulse raced. Gold it was, for certain-sure.

I swallowed hard, shoved my sleeves to my elbows and plunged my pan into the stream. A shiver flumed down my spine and I sucked in lungfuls of pine-scented breeze. The stream's indescribable cold pierced every pore of my bare flesh like needles. I gritted my teeth to keep them from chattering.

Sediment slopped over the pan's far lip. I shook it as Dick had demonstrated. The current whisked away the entire dredge.

"Swear and be damned, Abigail. You got all the grace of a three-legged musk ox. Take her slow, 'til you get the hang of this dance."

"But it looked so easy when you did it."

"God save me from greenhorns," he moaned, tipping his slouch hat to his eyebrows. "Hell, it ought to. I've been panning mud since afore you was born."

Dusky blue shadows poured down the mountains before I managed to sluice out most of the sediment while hoarding a pinch of flakes.

Between the four of us, we'd hardly gained enough gold to buy cigars to celebrate our discovery, but our spirits rose like smoke from the campfire.

Bone-weariness and the biting cold should have driven us into our tents. Instead, we sat huddled in blankets, faces burnished copper by the flames, backsides perched on logs.

"Garrett, I don't think I ever told you the world's best fish story . . ." Dick started.

"Yeah, you have, about a hun—"

" 'Twas on the Yuba River, that's in Californee, you know, that this prospector name of Jim Crow found hisself damn near starving.

"Ol' Jim waded into the river like a griz and commenced to catch hisself a fat salmon. Boiled that monster, gulped it down, then lo and behold, spied gold flakes shining pretty as you please at the bottom of the cookpot. Afore you know it, miners was dredging color at two thousand dollars a pan. I'll swan, ain't nobody never gigged a fish what tasted near as good as ol' Jim's lucky salmon."

"Aw, did that really happen, Garrett?" I asked.

"Heard Dick tell it enough times, sounds like gospel to me."

"I don't suppose," Ransom said, "that there's any use hoping for that kind of luck here."

"Can't never tell, boy. Me and Garrett's heard of men washing fifty feet apart. One strikes pay dirt and the other could sluice to China and find nothing but dirt-dirt."

Muscle spasms, like knife blades, stabbed between my shoulders and throbbed down my arms, forcing me to sit up straighter. They should have forced me into my bedroll, but I didn't want to miss a lick of the yarning.

"I guess it's silly for Ransom and me to be in such a hurry. You've prospected half your life waiting for a bonanza."

"The hell you say. I've scraped God knows how many thousands of dollars outta the ground."

Ransom cut in before I got the chance. "Then why are you as busted as the rest of us?"

Garrett threw his head back and laughed. "Because gold spends a sure sight easier than it finds, right, Dick?"

"Partly," he said, climbing to his feet. Stove-up joints crackled like the fire's tinder. "You youngsters might not believe it, but it truly ain't the finding that's kept these territories crawling with humanity for twenty years. It's the looking."

He turned toward his tent and Garrett stood to follow suit.

"Dick, wait," I blurted. "I don't understand."

"Better if you never do." The corners of his eyes crinkled with a half-smile. "I ain't much for book learning, but as I recollect, Columbus didn't scuttle his boat after he found this hunk of real estate. No, that old salt kept venturing out, searching for a bigger one."

Cogitating his final remark, I watched the skinny sage disappear behind his tent flap. Papa would have liked Dick enormously, and oh, what grand lies they'd have swapped.

Though I'd heard my father's repertoire a thousand times, like Dick, he had an instinctive, almost musical flair for inserting pauses, crescendos, and sharp notes where they'd have the most effect, which his daughter had not inherited.

"Justice is neither blind nor unfair," Papa had repeatedly maintained. "Upon my arrest at the cusp of my fifteenth birthday for saluting that landmark event with an equal number of pistol shots, the magistrate—a man of formidable character and intelligence, as I soon learned—levied a fine of ten dollars, plus two bits.

"While I accepted the ten-dollar punishment without question, the additional two bits gave me pause. In answer to my humble inquiry, the judge explained that the assessment was affixed to pay for the drink he would have enjoyed had my rambunctiousness not forced him to take leave of his seat at the saloon."

Justice to Papa's story, however, would not be done had I tried relating it to Dick. Given the choice, I'd have swapped my physical resemblance to Papa for a fraction of his oratorical artistry. Better yet, been visited by both.

I'd forgotten Ransom was still sitting beside me until he said, "Dick should have been a politician. He's pretty good at talking around questions without answering them."

"Oh, he answered, in his own way," I replied.

"Well, I can't make any sense of it."

Angling sideward to face him, I winced when my entire body protested the movement. "Lord, I may have to crawl to my tent."

"I can fix that. Ease around with your back to me."

"What?"

Ransom nudged my elbow. "Do as you're told . . . that's a good girl."

Through three shirts, a heavy coat, and a wool blanket, Ransom's strong fingers lazily kneaded away the soreness, the remedy equal parts rapture and agony. I closed my eyes, letting my head swing to and fro like a rag doll's.

"Had I known that this was the way to your heart," he said, "I'd have offered my services a long time ago."

That certainly raised my eyelids a trifle. I had no idea how to respond. Not having bathed for over two weeks and sleeping in the same clothes I traveled in, I hardly considered myself prime for ravishing—if that was what my masseur had in mind.

Putting an end to his ministrations by bidding him good night occurred to me, but lawsy, those glorious hands were working miracles on my back.

"Christ, Abigail. Am I so horrid that you won't even talk to me? I've done everything but knock you down trying to get your attention."

"What do you mean, my attention? For heaven's sake, Ransom, we're on a prospecting expedition, not stepping out together."

He scrambled around and knelt in front of me. "Is there any law against a man being enormously attracted to his business partner?"

I couldn't help chuckling at his earnest expression. It died in my throat when I met those blazing sapphire eyes. A strange flutter, like a kitten's paw, batted at my insides. "I'm not so sure there shouldn't be."

He gained his feet, reached down, and pulled me to mine. "I aim to make you glad there isn't, dear lady."

I thought he was going to kiss me and hadn't decided if I'd let him when he steered me toward my tent and wished me a restful night's sleep.

Squirming, drawing up my knees, and generally trying to achieve comfort and warmth inside my drafty peak of canvas, the realization of what I'd missed most since Papa died struck me as hard as lightning bludgeons a tree.

Without him, there was no shared history, no easy familiarity to depend on, no anchor to cling to. Suddenly among strangers, every mood, everything I said or did, required an explanation or a justification to those who didn't know me from Adam's off-ox. Or I, them.

I remembered telling Garrett that all I knew how to be was Maximilian Fiske's daughter, and that I really wasn't even that anymore. Well, those words spoke volumes I hadn't truly understood myself.

It's an unfettered Abigail Fiske that must make her way in this world now. She'd always be her father's daughter, but there was a far sight more to the old girl than that.

After all, it wasn't my paternity that Ransom Halsey got all calf-eyed over, was it?

May. Saturday, 4th, 1861

*Cold and snowing this morning. I went
down to creek and struck a trail. I saw
two deer once about 400 yards off, but it
was so late that I was obliged to give
them up.*

I awakened convinced that I'd never be warm
again. Gladly, I'd have bartered what scant
chance I had of a heavenly afterlife for a little
hellfire and brimstone.

Beyond Ransom's chuffy snores and Dick's
spatula scraping flapjacks from the skillet, the
world was a white-shrouded tomb. Low-hanging,
leaden clouds flattened the mountains like
squaw's teeth worn to nubs from chewing hides.

My mood was darker than the cup of scalding
brew I now clutched between mittened hands. I
wanted to go home, remembering with a wistful
sigh that I had none to go to.

We had planned to move on today, as the creek's precious handsel had dwindled faster than a doxie's virtue. According to Garrett, washing less than an ounce of gold per partner per day was a slow, sure route to bankruptcy.

Heading upland toward the treasure's source held more promise, so said the veterans I accompanied. Two years ago, almost to the day, a Georgian by the name of John Gregory, a blustery no-account by reputation, lucked upon the fabulous lode now bearing his name at the mouth of a narrow side gulch near Clear Creek.

No less a personage than Horace Greeley visited the booming site a month later. His breathless reportage reprinted in newspapers all across the country spurred Papa's and many thousand other pulses to a gallop.

Such legends set golden dreams to dancing in my sleep, but foul weather made a surly traveling companion. We'd tarry where our tents were staked and wood and water were plentiful until Providence deigned to favor us.

I heard footfalls crunch behind me, but still jumped when Garrett inquired, "Do you have cartridges to fit that Sharps?"

The urge to gasp coquettishly proved irresistible. "Why, mercy sakes, no. If I did, I might be sorely tempted to shoot something with it."

Squatted beside his open-air cookstove, Dick

cackled and shook his head. Garrett merely shifted his weight and glared. "It's just not your nature to answer a simple question straight, is it?"

"Nor is it yours to give me credit for having a brain between these dainty ears."

"That's not true."

"Oh? Then tell me, if I were a man, would it have even crossed your mind to ask whether I had ammunition for my rifle?"

His lips parted, then clamped shut in a thin line. I didn't much like myself at that moment, but I didn't like Garrett's habit of treating me like a wilting lily, either.

Instinctively, I knew he'd been raised a proper gentleman with rules of conduct regarding the fairer sex as ingrained as the multiplication tables, whereas I'd grown up as free of social convention as a clump of bunchgrass.

Time and subtle guidance would surely enlighten him eventually. The latter was hardly my strong suit, but I had plenty of the former at my disposal.

"She's got you dead to rights, Garrett," Dick chimed in. "Might as well wave your hanky and be done with it."

I winked at the older man, then said, "No need for that, Garrett. The reason behind your question'll do."

The towering inquisitor appeared a mite sheepish. "I reckoned you might want to put that cannon to use, that's all. We'd welcome some fresh meat for supper." With an ornery grin, he tacked on, "If you're agreeable."

I answered with one of my own, absolutely delighted to have something to do besides watch Dick char his breakfast and count snowflakes as they fell. "I'll be ready in two shakes."

"No hurry. Finish your coffee while I muster Ransom out of his bedroll."

"And why must you do that?" I inquired suspiciously.

"Because it'd be plumb stupid for you or anybody else to hie off all by your lonesome."

"But Ransom doesn't own a rifle, much less know how to shoot one."

"The dude doesn't know blossom rock from his hindquarters, either," Garrett countered, "which is what Dick and I'll be scouting for while you're gone."

I didn't know what blossom rock was, either, but before I exposed my ignorance on the subject, he was plowing through the snow toward Ransom's tent.

"Damned if you two aren't like puppies tussling for a front teat," Dick teased.

With a flip of my wrist, cold dregs arced from my cup and splattered against a tree trunk. I stowed the battered tinware behind the canvas fly and slid my rifle and a leather pouch of shells from beneath my tousled blankets.

"Tired of hearing us bicker, eh?"

"Naw. It's more entertaining than picking nits outta my whiskers, long as you don't turn it on me."

"And I won't, since you never act like I'm constantly in danger of succumbing to the vapors. Lord above, Dick, haven't I done my share so far?"

He grunted, chewing a wad of flapjack as fast as he was able. A gulp, followed by a swig of coffee, brought forth a reply. "I got no complaints. Trouble is, you expect Garrett to treat you like one of the boys, which it's obvious you ain't. Shouldn't fault him for that."

Seesawing his fork's edge across another chunk, he peered up from under his hat brim. " 'Spect you really wouldn't want him to anyhow, truth be known."

He bowed his head to take another bite, leaving me staring at the rumpled felt crown that sheltered an amazingly perceptive mind. There were more than monetary enrichments to be gleaned from Dick's acquaintanceship.

Swinging the Sharps' barrel away from civilization, I jerked back the brass side-hammer to be sure I had lead at my disposal. The carbine was as well balanced and dependable as it was handsome, but I'd have treasured it regardless.

Back in Hays, Kansas, Papa'd mucked out stalls at Crookshank's Livery and tended bar at night to buy it for my twentieth birthday. To spend that sweat-earned cash on a couple of westbound stage tickets would have been more practical, so therefore, it never occurred to him. Fingering the metal button embedded in the stock and embossed with my initials, I was thankful now that it had not.

Along the first mile of our foraging expedition, Ransom staggered behind me, alternately rubbing sleep from his eyes and crashing through deadfalls as quietly as a stampeding buffalo herd. There'd be something besides beans on our plates tonight only if we were fortunate enough to encounter a stone-deaf grizzly.

From time to time, I paused to notch a tree to mark our trail. The bark of a mammoth oak likely older than Jesus seemed ironclad. I was struggling to release the knife when Ransom's hand closed over mine.

"Allow me."

The blade jerked free, toppling me backward against his chest. Ransom's other arm curled around my waist, hugging me tight, his cheek rubbing the side of my head like a housecat caressing its owner's leg.

His hair smelled faintly of bay rum and wood smoke, a wonderfully masculine aroma. I let myself melt into his embrace, wondering, abstractly, as I had during our previous romancings, how he stayed so dashingly *clean* despite the trail's privations. And how he made me feel as desirable as an Atlanta belle.

The knife slipped from my grasp and chinked into the snow. Gently, Ransom turned me around. His lips teased mine, then claimed them for a long, sweetly sensual kiss that left me trembling and greedy for more.

He satisfied that craving until I was breathless and almost too dizzy to stand. Sly devil. Those eyes glistened, knowing full well the fire he'd kindled in me.

"If only this hillside were strewn with wildflowers, I'd pleasure you until you begged for mercy."

I pushed away a step, smiling coyly. "Oh, no, you would not, Mr. Halsey. My virtue isn't that easily won."

In an instant, his lusty expression faded to pensive uncertainty. "I love you, Abigail. Don't you know that by now? I want to spend the rest of my life with you."

Birds chattered irritably from lofty branches. The stream blundered into rocks and gnarled roots in its mad rush to join the South Platte or the Arkansas. My senses churned with sights, smells, and sounds, but my mind was blank.

"I don't know what to say, Ransom."

He grinned lopsidedly, as people do when they're sure they're about to make fools of themselves, yet hopeful the listener will forgive them. "I love you, too, would be a nice start."

I took his hands in mine and squeezed them. "I can't. I mean, I don't know if . . ."

A throaty chuckle rumbled up his throat. "Haven't swept you off your feet, eh? Ah, you're an honest woman, darlin' Abigail, and beautiful, intelligent, and strong willed to boot."

He reached down and grabbed the knife, carefully sheathing it in my belt's leather scabbard. "You'll succumb to my charms someday and do me the honor of becoming my wife."

"Pretty sure of yourself, aren't you?"

Settling an arm around my shoulders, he said, "Sure of how I feel about you, yes. And when my ardor captivates your heart, I'll be the luckiest man alive."

"There are some who'd argue that. Strenuously."

"Let 'em," he scoffed, waving a hand as if shooing flies from a window screen. "We're going to find us the whoppingest gold mine this territory's ever seen. There'll be a wedding band crafted from the first dazzling proceeds and we'll live like royalty, happily ever after, sharing that fabulous mountain of money."

An eerie concert of past and present played in my mind. Their voices were different: Ransom's deep and hypnotic, and at the last, Papa's whiskey-burnt tenor rasping like spent cornstalks in the wind. But a gossamer trace of the naive, invincible dreamer lilted in both.

We started out again, holding on to each other like tipsy sailors on shore leave. Cloven tracks and fresh scat held the promise of game ahead, yet not a speck of dinner-on-the-hoof graced our path.

Crimson and pink tinges lacing the dingy clouds warned that day's end was approaching. After doubling back for camp, a majestic eleven-point buck's headdress pivoted above a brambled thatch. A second, smaller deer stood rigid at his side.

I tugged the hem of Ransom's coat, signaling for a halt. He must've understood the meaning behind my scowl as he squelched a surprised grunt.

Even for my trusty Sharps, the distance between hunter and the hunted was too great. I couldn't see that pair of glossy black noses twitch after our scent, but knew they did. Seconds later, the beasts spooked gracefully into the underbrush.

"Why didn't you shoot?"

I aimed an exasperated look over my shoulder. "Because the best I could've done at this range is scare one of them to death."

"Sorry." He scrambled to catch up with me. "Being raised in Philadelphia didn't lend many opportunities for blood sport."

I'd have taken mild exception to that remark if I weren't actively mourning the loss of venison steaks. Ransom meant well and certainly tried his best to learn the skills sadly lacking from a privileged, citified upbringing.

"No insult intended, Ransom, but what possessed a well-to-do, university-educated man like you to come west? This hardscrabble country slays as many characters as it builds."

He sunk his hands in his pockets and gazed straight ahead. "My father owns the biggest steel smelter on the eastern seaboard. His only expectation for my three older sisters was marrying well, preferably to men who exceeded our station in life. I, however, was groomed practically from birth to take over his domain."

Snorting bitterly, he continued. "Father didn't bother asking whether I gave a damn about any part of it, which assuredly I did not. The day I made those feelings known, he threw me out the door by my braces, tossed a handful of shinplasters on the heap, and ordered me off his property. Permanently."

He shrugged, adding, "From what I'd read, Colorado seemed as good a place as any to start from scratch."

"Didn't your mother—"

"Never knew her. She died in childbirth." Ransom laughed, but there was no humor in it. "But I'd bet Silvianna, my stepmother, brought out the Baccarat to toast my disinheritance."

Like Ransom, I knew what it was like to grow up semi-orphaned. When I was about seven Papa told me why I didn't have a mother to kiss the sting from my scraped knees or rock me in her lap just because she liked the warmth of my skinny frame pressed to her rounded belly and bosom.

I remembered the whiskey-sour breath and fat tears wobbling down his cheeks as Papa blamed himself for shredding my mother's heart with cruel words and glowering silences. A length of hemp wrapped around a barn's center beam afforded her an escape from tyranny.

I hadn't understood then, and probably never would. The man who cherished me more than life itself was not the ogre he professed himself to be, once upon a time.

Ransom and I pushed onward in the waning, dusky light until spying the gray tendrils vining upward from our creekside campfire. Our half-encircled, saggy tents seemed like old friends extending their hospitality, although I grimaced a tad, guessing how the men silhouetted by the flames would react to our empty-handed return.

Game was scarce, that was a fact, but Ransom and I'd spent more time stalking each other than hidebound provisions. Garrett would probably deduce as much, which, oddly, bothered me a jot.

I glanced at Ransom striding along at my elbow. A lazy smile, like a lad who'd eaten his fill of gingersnaps and sweet milk, spread across his sculptured features.

"I do love you, Abigail," he murmured. "And how desperately I need you to love me."

May. Friday, 10th, 1861

*Started from camp early. Stoophy fell off
the bank into the Blue River. I came
within an ace of drowning. Cool and
snowy.*

Despite his age and abiding affection for tan-
glefoot and cigars, Dick's lungs were as hardy as
fireplace bellows. As for me, each breath felt as
if it were drawn through a feather pillow.

Heading ever westward, the snow-packed terrain wasn't terribly difficult to traverse other
than the fact that every slanted step raised me a
half-foot closer to the Almighty's lofty kingdom.

About midday, we came upon the Blue River,
an aptly named freshet if ever there was one. Its
current, swift as a runaway locomotive, wouldn't
tempt a lunatic to cross. Naturally, Dick and
Garrett fell to debating how best to do precisely that.

I asked Ransom to share my stash of cold biscuits and raisins while our partners stroked their chin whiskers and plotted our watery demise.

Offering him a palm's weight of fruit, he grimaced and shook his head. "I'm not hungry enough to eat bullets, darlin'. Thanks anyway."

"They're a mite frozen, but I've seen what ugly things scurvy does to a body. Bleeding gums, limbs bloated to bursting. I wouldn't chance it, if I were you."

"Abigail . . ."

I dumped the wrinkled pellets into Ransom's hand and hastened to answer Dick's summons.

"I'm fixing to scout a ford up yonder," he said, "and don't need no mule along slowing me down. Garrett'll lead Remus. Think you can handle Stoophy?"

The animal eyed me skeptically. He snorted as if he savvied his owner's question and wasn't fond of the idea. I was enormously flattered to be entrusted with Dick's most prized possession, yet was quite aware of the beast's numerous eccentricities, which included mistaking bystanders' appendages for ripe fodder.

"I'll, uh, do my best, but maybe Ransom'd be—"

Garrett grunted. "He can't hardly get himself from here to there," he replied in a low voice.

"I'm not partial to risking our grub and tools to a tinhorn."

A better woman than I would have defended her suitor's honor, not grinned like a rabid dog and nodded her acceptance. Knowing that Ransom did not enjoy cajoling our pack animals' cooperation justified my treachery somewhat.

Dick had already vanished around a bend. After letting the mules drink their fill, Garrett led Remus at the point position, with me and Stoophy at flank and Ransom at drag.

Every few feet, my dappled charge brayed and reared back as if trying to wrest the come-alongs from my clutches.

"Switch to the outside and stay with him," Garrett called over his shoulder. "He's just riled because he's behind Remus instead of in front."

I did as I was told. To demonstrate that my stubbornness at least equaled his, I took a firm grip on Stoophy's halter. The mule tried to whip his head away, but I held him firm. Both ears laid back as flat as shotgun barrels, but Stoophy didn't truck with me further.

In time, the bank narrowed to a boggy ledge. Fir branches crowded our path, their flocked, needled fingertips brushing man and beast as they passed. I eased my grasp slightly to step up on a flat-topped boulder resting like a toppled tombstone at the river's edge.

Stoophy took instant, vengeful advantage of my perilous stance. When he butted me sideward, my boots slipped on the slick surface. The mule stumbled, his heavy pack throwing him off balance. We both careened into the water, screaming. I was helpless against the current. One shoulder slammed into a boulder. Beneath the surface, jagged rocks tore at my legs like monstrous teeth. I flailed leaden arms, fighting to keep my head above water.

"*Move*, you stupid bastard," I heard Garrett yell. "Run downstream and catch her!"

Ransom trotted along the bank, shrieking, "I can't swim! I can't swim!"

Icy water rushed into my mouth, choking me. Again and again, I was sucked under. A thick, green-gray fog descended, blurring my vision. As darkness closed around me, I glimpsed an uprooted tree canting out from the bank.

I raised my arms to shag it. A swell lifted me upward. The trunk poleaxed me just below the ribs. Bile scalded my throat and gushed from my nose and mouth.

The tree bobbed beneath me. Hands clutched my collar and the seat of my trousers. I was carried to safety like a sack of potatoes and laid on my side on blessedly dry ground.

Gingerly, my savior eased me onto my back. I squinted up into Garrett's sheet-white face.

"Are you all right, little gal?"

"Cold," was all I could manage through chattering teeth.

"Get every blanket we've got, Halsey," he barked. "Now!"

Within minutes, Ransom bent over me, piling woolens one atop another. My shivering and the pain roaring through my body with every tremble only worsened. I felt dizzy, nauseous, wretched.

"Abigail, if you don't get out of those wet clothes, you're gonna freeze to death," Garrett said softly. "Gotta check for broken bones and such, too. Here, I'll help—"

"The *hell* you will," Ransom bellowed.

Garrett's fists clenched as he stood and whirled. "You gutless puke. She damned near died once already because of you."

He cocked an arm and belted Ransom in the jaw. The last thing I remember was Garrett's target pinwheeling backward and crumpling into a snowbank.

May. Saturday, 11th, 1861

*Was very sick all night and today. Thought
my head would burst. Arapahoe Indians
camped with us and we fed them.*

The sun washed the grubby canvas peaked above
me with a pale amber glow. I vaguely remembered awakening off and on throughout the
night, heaving and retching every drop of the
Blue River I'd swallowed.

My hand investigated a pair of unfamiliar cor-
duroy breeches and a flannel shirt. Donations, I
presumed, from my partners' knapsacks.

I decided to banish thoughts of Garrett strip-
ping me to the skin completely from my mind.
He'd surely seen scores of naked, supremely en-
dowed women in his life and was probably quite
bored by my sodden denouement. The
scoundrel.

Without raising my throbbing head, I peered

down the trough my limbs and feet formed under the blankets. Either yesterday's misadventure had completely unhinged me or there were four Indians squatted around our campfire palavering with Dick and Garrett.

I shut my eyes, reopening them slowly. The raven-haired quartet reappeared, one's long mane decorated with a turkey beard roach secured at the crown by a braided strand.

All were ruggedly attractive in a primitive sort of way, and dressed in poncholike affairs sewn from mountain sheep skins, rawhide-soled moccasins, and leggings fringed with horsehair.

Most maidens of my acquaintance would have shed water at the mere thought of an Indian, but during his doctor phase, Papa and I were welcome visitors to several tribal communities. We did, however, take the precaution of departing our hosts' village before the medicinal benefits of Papa's nostrums took full effect.

A shadow fell across the open tent fly, followed by a face craning around the fold. Smudgy crescents beneath Ransom's eyes matched the angry polt on his stubbled jawline.

"You're awake?"

"I must be. I seldom dream of fleece-clad savages coming to tea."

He patted my leg, his smile at best a woebegone grimace. "Don't talk, just listen, though there aren't any words to tell you how sorry I am for—"

"Oh, Ransom, you're not to blame. No one is."

He continued as if he hadn't heard me. "I was too terrified for myself to save the only woman I've ever loved."

"Bullfeathers. All that matters is that neither of us ended up with a cross planted above our brow."

"Then you don't despise me?"

I tried wriggling into a sitting position and bit my lip to stifle a groan. A hammer walloped my brain like an anvil. Myriad aches at my midsection paled in comparison.

" 'Course not." I laid back on the wadded tow sacks that served as my pillow. "What I want to hear is what happened after, uh—"

"After Garrett bid me an abrupt good night?"

"Hey, Halsey," Dick called. "Come'n get this special-made coffee. It'll fix what ails her."

As Ransom complied, Dick hunkered down on his stump perch and hollered as if deafness was my primary affliction. "Glad you're coming around, gal. Dinner'll be ready directly."

The Indians leaned sideways, bobbing like chickens on the strut trying to get a better look at me. None seemed particularly taken by my charms. I waved an acknowledgment, surprised that my sore belly started rumbling at the mention of food.

Ransom eased inside again, crawling on all threes—one hand occupied with balancing a tin cup without sloshing its contents.

I took a sip and promptly gagged. The vile brew blazed a trail clear to my gullet. "What's Dick trying to do? Put me out of my misery permanently?"

Ransom shrugged. "No better painkiller than a dose of Taos Lightning, says he. Strikes hard, fast, and leaves nothing standing."

The fumes from that criminal ruination of good coffee almost brought tears to my eyes. But I couldn't deny the exceptionally pain-free condition Dick had achieved a couple of times since we'd left Denver City.

Gamely, I gulped a hearty swallow, then croaked, "Start talking."

With his lengthy frame settled half in and half out of my humble quarters, he began by admitting, "There isn't much to tell, really. Dick and I made camp while Garrett, er, tended to your injuries. That you didn't suffer any broken bones is an absolute miracle."

"What about Stoophy?" I asked, fearing his response.

"Scraped, bruised, and meaner than ever. I guess the water was shallow enough for him to get his footing before the current carried him away. One knee's swelled pretty badly, but our Arapahoe guests cooked some pine resin and fashioned a poultice."

"Has it helped?"

"Seems to've." He chuckled. "Only they had to stir up another one for the Injun doing the doctoring. Stoophy nipped him right smartly on his shoulder."

"Lord above, if that mule were a man, somebody'd have hanged him long ago." I yawned, my eyelids growing as heavy as counterweights. "You'd think he'd have the sense to be grateful."

Ransom's expression mirrored his displeasure. "As if feeding the savages several pounds of our provisions isn't gratitude enough. I can't understand their heathen gibberish, but Dick said they wandered in fresh from a battle with the Utes. A losing one, I'd say."

His voice faded as if he were speaking from a great distance. "At least if the redskins are busy massacring each other, they won't be harrying us whites. Except for free meals."

The next thing I knew, someone was insistently nudging my shoulder. A heavenly aroma filled my nostrils.

"Dinner is served, ma'am," Garrett said. "All you've got to do is open your mouth, close it, and chew."

After I propped my much clearer head with one elbow, he delivered a spoonful of johnnycake soaked in a rich, tangy broth. "Figured my famous rabbit stew'd taste pretty good. Lucky for you, a plump one hopped by right where I was aiming and the Arapahoes skedaddled before I got the pot on the fire."

"Lawsy, it's ambrosia, Garrett—" He interrupted my praise with another helping.

"At risk of being lambasted for bossing you around, hush up and enjoy the first food you've eaten since yesterday. You and Ransom prattled on for far too long this morning."

I nodded meekly and opened wide for another bite.

"That's a girl. Now, I know you feel like you've been drug behind a fast horse for a mile or three, but you're gonna be fine."

His angled features tensed, as if carved from flint rock. "Coulda been so damn much worse it scares me just thinking about it."

I held up my hand to halt his caretaking temporarily. "True enough, but I don't want my accident to cause bad blood between you and Ransom."

"It hasn't. Never liked him, anyway. There's something about pukes that always set my neck hairs on end."

"I'll thank you not to use that term again, Garrett Collingsworth. It's not only vulgar, it's—it's *incorrect*. Ransom hails from Pennsylvania, not Missouri."

"The hell he does."

Another dose of dinner waggled beneath my nose. Rather than inhale it, I snapped at the lump like a trout snaffles an insect.

Grateful as I was to him for plucking me from the Blue River's clutches, that Garrett could switch from a gentle giant to an insufferable know-it-all in the span of a pulse beat was incredibly aggravating.

The rest of the meal passed in a taut silence. When the pickings got slim, he said gruffly, "There's more in the pot if you want it."

"I've had plenty, thank you. And thank you for taking the trouble of feeding it to me."

"No trouble."

"I reckon I'll be on my feet by tomorrow."

"Probably," he agreed as he backed through the fly. "If you're not, we'll rig a travois to take you to the new camp."

"What new camp? Did Dick find a ford?" I wouldn't have admitted it, but I'd have rather broken bread with Phil the Cannibal than brave that river again so soon.

"Nope. He found something better."

I waited for him to expound on that tantalizing statement, whereas, being closely related to

Stoophy, he refused to do so until I all but bellowed, *"What?"*

His lips parted and curved in a decidedly feral manner. "Oh, just a gulch that appears to have some gold sprinkled thereabouts."

May. Tuesday, 14th, 1861

Went to work this morning, two of us washing, one gone over to a Gulch to claim it for prospecting purposes. We sluiced awhile and then crossed the branch and commenced to sink a hole. After dinner, a man came to us and told us that this was his claim. This has been an awfull week. Clear and pleasant.

A dark side to democracy became clear to me this morning. The majority ruled that I was too frail for any prospecting, but recovered enough to gather wood, tend the fire, and cook dinner.

Honestly, I didn't mind taking my turn at the housekeeping chores, particularly since the boys had treated me so kindly when I was abed. It was more a sense of being left out of the fun, like a tenth man on a baseball team.

My mood lightened appreciably when Garrett

gave Ransom the responsibility of staking our company's four contiguous claims, plus another entitlement termed a "discovery" claim.

At first Ransom sneered, as if a cruel joke were being played. Garrett continued by instructing, "Pace each at a hundred feet long following the gulch's meanderings, by fifty feet wide."

With that, his apprentice all but swooned.

Afraid that Garrett might be the type who considered compliments the same as calling him a milksop, I didn't tell him how admirable I thought his bygones-be-bygones gesture was. Instead, I began preparing a sumptuous meal, although beans, as always, would be the featured entree.

At the mouth of the gulch, Garrett and Dick took up their chore of hollowing a log for a makeshift sluice. They'd spent the better part of two days hewing it out, whereas building a plank one would have taken mere hours had our means been equal to lumber's dear price.

Thunks of their single-blade adzes kept tempo with Dick's retelling, for the umpteenth time, how he'd found gold literally at his feet while I was undergoing my unexpected bath in the Blue River.

"There I was, kinda surveying the terrain whilst I irrigated it. Lo and behold, I looked down to check my aim and damned if I wasn't standing smack-dab in a patch of blossom rock.

"Them bits of white quartz a-busting with orangey veins . . . why, 'twas the purtiest thing I've seen this side of Dolly LaDue's sporting house."

Like a well-rehearsed actor, Garrett drawled his now-customary line on cue. "I've heard of fellows that pissed off a fortune, but you're the first I've ever known that pissed *on* one."

"Ain't all that got pissed on . . ."

Rather than subject myself to more of the same and worse, I closed my ears and busied myself mixing rice and raisins for a batch of spotted pup.

I'd caught glimpses of Ransom trudging all over our snowy El Dorado, hacking away brush and splashing back and forth across the stream bisecting the gulch to place stakes precisely where they belonged.

When he finally sauntered into camp, he was as grubby as a derelict, with twigs sprouting from his hair like antlers. He tossed a mallet and extra stakes aside. "Got any water to spare?"

"I'd say you've earned a dipper's-worth." I used its handle to crack the bucket's icy skim, then filled the bowl. "Hard as you were going at it, I'd swear I saw you grinning as wide as a boy astride his first pony."

"Probably due to what I was thinking about while I stepped off those measurements."

"That there's three feet to a yard, I hope."

He graced me with a wry look. "I was ciphering, all right, but something a lot more grand than that."

Silently, I wondered how it'd become my lot in life to ask "What?" in response to a damnably large percentage of my partners' statements. But it had, so I did.

He raised my chin and kissed me. Before I could chastise him for taking such public liberties, he answered, "I was thinking about how if you were my wife, fully half of this claim would belong to us."

I'd certainly never featured it in those terms and wouldn't have, save Ransom's prompting. Lord above, what *would* I do with my quarter's proceeds, much less a half?

Seldom having more than enough money to keep the wolf from the door and on occasion lacking that, I couldn't imagine what unbridled wealth would be like.

Gewgaws lusted after by many of my gender held little appeal for me. Acquiring the latest Paris fashions, a diamond tiara, and box seats at an opera house were not worth traipsing Colorado's high country to have.

Having unlimited funds at my disposal would

probably require a week or two's adjustment, but I reckoned I could become accustomed to it.

"Why, Ransom Halsey, if I didn't know you were hopelessly in love with me, I'd think you wanted to marry me for my money."

"That's not all I'm after, darlin'." He ogled me lecherously, his tongue tracing his lips. "But I suppose the same could be said of you."

"No, it can't. I haven't accepted your proposal."

From the corner of my eye, I saw Dick and Garrett ambling toward us and turned to give the beans a final stir. Ransom bent over my shoulder. "You haven't said no, either, my love."

Within minutes, snorts and grunts like hungry hogs falling to their slops rent the air. I hadn't finished my first helping before I was doling out seconds, then thirds. There wouldn't be enough scraps left to feed a nest of robins.

"What'd you do to them beans, gal?" Dick groaned, leaning back against our piled stores. "Best I ever et."

"Added a pinch of salt and pepper," I replied drolly.

An iron pot tolled like a church bell as Garrett scraped it with a ladle. "You kinda scanted us on the spotted pup, though. And I only got five biscuits."

"No offense, Dick," Ransom joined in, "but I wish Abigail'd do the cooking from now on."

My delight at their compliments diminished instantly. "Oh, no, you don't. I'm not about to trade my gold pan for a frying pan."

The three grinned at each other, then Dick said slyly, "I reckon we oughta put it to a vote, don't you, boys?"

Garrett nodded. "That's the American way of settling things, sure enough."

On the outside chance that they were serious, I said, "You know, I'm suddenly in the mood to make you boys an apple pie for supper." Gazing toward the trees where the mules were tethered, I added, "And I know just where I'll get the apples to do it."

"Hear that?" Dick muttered with mock disgust. "Women're meaner'n a nest of rattlesnakes. 'Least them varmints give fair warning afore they strike."

Garrett winked at me. "Amen to that. And God help us all if the gals ever get the vote."

Tinware rattled like thunder in the empty washtub. The fire needed tending; there was water to fetch and set to boiling. Our ever-thickening pot of Arbuckle's could bear replenishing. Lawsy, what a shame I was too weak to do any real work.

I'd like to have credited my cooking skill for inspiring Garrett's increasing goodwill toward Ransom. Whatever the cause, he shocked my beau for the second time that day by ordering him to depart immediately for Humbug City to register our claims.

"You want me to represent the company?"

Garrett hitched his britches over his swollen belly. "Any reason why you shouldn't?"

"Jesus Chri—no! Just point me the right direction and I'm good as there."

"Strike out east 'bout two miles," Dick answered. "If'n you meet up with a creek, you've done missed it already. Humbug ain't got more'n about twenty pioneers."

"Bet it isn't long before somebody gets hellbent to plat it," Garrett observed. "Soon as one does, half the population'll be running for district representative."

"Damn straight on that."

Ransom hesitated a moment. "Who do I say's claiming it? Collingsworth and Company?"

Dick's face fell as blank as a schoolhouse slate on Saturday. "By God, we plumb neglected to name the danged thing."

"How about The Morning Dew?" Garrett suggested. "That's what was spilling when you found it."

I banged the lid down on the coffeepot. "Have you forgotten there's a lady present?"

Obviously they had, for Dick countered, "Prissiest moniker I ever heard. Anyhow, 'twas afternoon, not morning, big fella."

"Good thing, too. If it'd been earlier, you might've been taking a—"

"Ga-rr-et-t . . ."

"Yes, ma'am?"

Dick smacked fist to palm like a gavel. "Got it!" Raising his arm and pantomiming a downright blasphemous sign of the cross, he declared, "I baptize thee The Gee Whiz in the name of Lewis and Clark what discovered this territory, and Arbuckle's Best that brung me here."

I considered throwing a rollicking hissy, but why bother when my partners were almost splitting their britches laughing? Boys will most certainly be boys, from birth until they're buried. As Lillith said, we weren't blessed with any alternatives.

"We'd better get to slogging before Abigail's ol' pickle-puss gets stuck, permanent." Dick handed Ransom a twine-tied cloth bag. "Get this assayed, too, and give the man the whole poke for his services. Probably won't keep him quiet, but he might think awhile afore he tells every mother's son where it came from."

At the rate he lit out, Ransom likely reached Humbug City before I finished scouring the mucky pots and pans. Reluctantly, I'd agreed to fix our evening meal so the other two could start digging a hole above the cache Dick had discovered. But, oh my, how I wanted to feel gold-veined pebbles sifting through my fingers instead of cornmeal.

Though neither had seen fit to explain the process to me, eavesdropping lent a degree of understanding. Tunneling into the gulch's silty wall should expose a heavier surface vein. They'd pitch the diggings by the shovel load into the log sluice, a flumelike affair with a drain slit at one end and small holes piercing its bottom. Buckets of water would then be poured down the sluice to rinse away the sediment, but not the larger chunks of blossom rock.

The *zwing*ing sound of shovels biting into frozen gravel grew louder as I neared the site where Dick and Garrett worked knee-deep in the snow. Contrasting with the sparkling white powder, the ragged oval they'd excavated looked like an ugly wound.

They'd placed the sluice a few feet behind them, an end propped and cradled by one of the mule's pack trees. Both men panted like plow oxen, vapor streaming from their lips.

Presently, Garrett sloshed water over their handiwork. Thin, rusty mud dribbled out the far end. He scrutinized the leavings for a moment, then picked up his shovel and plunged it into the deepening crevasse.

Little over a month ago, I'd thought panning for gold was an awfully hard way to earn a living. Watching my partners move a mountain one shovel at a time, I recalled what Dick had said when I'd grumbled about working so long for so little: "If'n you want to get rich fast and easy, gal, go rob a goddamned bank."

I was chuckling to myself when, from not ten feet behind me, came the distinctive clicks of a shotgun's hammers cocking back.

"Don't even sneeze, boy, or I'll blow your head clean off."

Garrett whirled. His eyes darted from me to a point beyond my left shoulder and back again. Only the shovel moved to nudge Dick with the tip.

The argonaut looked up. "What the . . ." His voice trailed away. "Do as you're told, er, Fiske."

I nodded, not wanting to betray my gender by speaking aloud.

"Which one of you's in charge?"

"I am," Garrett answered curtly.

"This man belong to your party?" Snow crunched as someone stepped forward. I turned my head slightly. Dried blood was caked beneath Ransom's nose and down his chin. A filthy rag was stuffed in his mouth, his hands tied behind his back.

"He does."

"Well, I'd warrant it takes fair-sized balls for you gents to jump a claim that just got filed yesterday mornin'."

"The hell you say! Rans—" Garrett paused. His tone was deadly flat when he finished with, "I scouted for stakes before I set ours."

"We didn't put none down yet, but we damn sure left our tools in plain sight. 'Course, they ain't where we left 'em, but that's the same as staking and don't tell me you didn't know it."

Garrett and Dick pegged Ransom with identical glares. Even I knew that according to miner's code, crossed picks and shovels indicated ownership as legally as a duly recorded claim. Hadn't Ransom ever bothered to listen when Garrett and Dick discussed such things?

"I'll take your word for it, mister," Garrett said gruffly. "We'll be packed and gone by daybreak."

"Not good enough," preceded a sickening thud. Ransom slammed into me, sending us both sprawling. "You got yourself an hour."

Garrett stalked over and rolled Ransom off me. He helped me to my feet and murmured, "Hold this shovel so's the bastard can't see your face. Break camp."

He then squatted to cut the rope binding Ransom's wrists, leaving him where he'd fallen.

Not a word was spoken as we gathered our belongings and loaded the mules. Twilight fell like a gray curtain in front of a monstrous stage. Surely we'd exceeded our deadline, but the silent sentry crouched against a cedar tree allowed us passage.

If not for clear skies, a bright moon, and the snow cover, we'd have walked blindly off the mountainside. Blazing fires had always protected us from night predators, so I'd never feared wolves howling from the shadows or the scuttles and thumps of unseen creatures feeding or bounding away from slavering enemies.

Now, traveling in near darkness, I jumped at the slightest rustle. Easing my Sharps from Remus's pack lent some measure of security.

Turning the rifle on our hateful intruder had occurred to me when I struck my tent. The brute force he applied certainly hadn't been necessary, yet it was senseless to start a fight. He had rights to the claim and we did not.

It was impossible to gauge how far we'd traveled. With trees becoming scarcer and weather-stunted, I knew we'd climbed high above the Blue River's domain.

Biting cold and weariness caused my head to commence throbbing again. I was about to swallow my pride and ask Garrett for a rest when he halted in a broad clearing.

"This'll do for tonight—what's left of it. No tents. Dick, get a fire going and cut boughs for under our bedrolls. Abigail, watch him and see he does it right."

"But—"

"I'm in no mood for arguing," he shot back. "Halsey, you and I are gonna unpack the mules."

The two younger men melted into the shadows, but anyone with pricked ears overheard what followed.

"Why'd you hide those tools, Halsey?"

"I didn't. I thought they'd been left behind a long time ago and just tossed them out of the way—"

"Uh-huh. You know how much that stuff costs. Why didn't you lug them to camp for us to use?"

"Swear to God, Garrett, I was going to after dinner. Forgot all about it when you sent me to Humbug City."

Except for our goods thumping to the ground, an ominous quiet descended. I understood Garrett's fury, yet I felt sorry for Ransom.

"That pilgrim scuffled you pretty rough, did he?"

Ransom groaned. "Bad enough. I think the bastard broke my nose."

"Hear me good, then, boy. You ever pull a stunt like that again and I'll kill ya."

May. Wednesday, 15th, 1861

*Warm when we started out. Had not got
a mile when it commenced to blow and
snow like everything. Very cold, the
awfullest wind I ever saw. Snow knee
deep. Snowing tonight like all the world.*

Snow clung to my lashes. Wind-driven flakes
pelted through eye-slits in the scarf wrapped
around my face. The swirling white horde addled
my sense of balance.

The storm erupted with incredible speed. At
dawn, we'd welcomed the sky's frothy overcast
because cloud cover captured the earth's heat
like a lid atop a Dutch oven. It was far from
balmy, but Old Man Winter had eased his grip
considerably. Even the mules stepped livelier
when we abandoned our makeshift camp.

Before two hours had elapsed, a stormy gloom
descended, almost blotting out the sun. On im-

pact, raindrops sealed everything they touched in icy cocoons. What had been a spry breeze howled into a demonic rage. With it, the torrential downpour clabbered into a blinding blizzard.

Both mules brayed in terror, shying from the swarming flakes.

"Dick, Ransom, wrap your scarfs over their eyes," Garrett shouted over the squall's roar. "Shorten their leads. Can't risk 'em breakin' loose."

"We're going on?" Ransom bellowed.

"We stay and we'll freeze to death," Garrett answered. "Abigail, up here."

The wind shoved at me from all directions as I slogged to the head of the line. Garrett cinched a rope around my waist, securing the other end around his own.

"Short lead for me, too?"

His bloodshot brown eyes caught mine for an instant. "Don't want to lose you, either."

Until Garrett adjusted his longer strides to mine, I jerked along behind him like a pull-toy on a string. Falling into a matched, swaying cadence, I entrusted my survival to my guide, eight feet of twisted hemp, and God.

The storm swallowed all sound but its own. I felt as if I were submerged in deep water. No matter how hard I struggled, I couldn't break the surface. The world beyond Garrett's broad back was a yawning, shadowy abyss.

The wind tore the breath from my throat. Without my mittened hands clamped over my mouth, I couldn't breathe. Onward I trudged, my lungs seared by the cold, thighs and calves cramping painfully and begging a moment's rest I knew would be denied.

Head bent against the wind, I counted steps in my mind. When I faltered over the tally, I'd start again at one, grateful for the deceptively small number.

Time and place lost all meaning. I have no idea how far or how long we walked, any more than I realized Garrett had stopped until I blundered into him.

"Cave," he said, pointing at a dark gape in the canyon's sheer embankment. His numb hands fumbled to unknot the rope. "We'll make for it."

Scattered boulders guarded the sanctuary. I stepped up and immediately fell to my knees. Tears sprang to my eyes, but this was no time to weep over bruises.

I crawled over the icy impediments and into the cave. It smelled of moss, wet fur, and scat, but didn't appear to be occupied. I could've slain a pack of wolves to claim it, if it had.

Garrett pulled me into his arms and held me

close. We sagged against each other, exhausted from our ordeal.

"I'll melt snow and set the pot to boiling, soon as the others get here," I murmured. "That'll thaw our bones in a—"

"We've lost them, Abigail. Somewhere a ways back."

I lurched from his embrace, my heart sliding into my boots. "Lost them? Where? When?"

He shook his head. "I don't know. One minute they were behind us, the next time I looked, they'd vanished."

"We've got to find them." I started for the entrance.

Garrett caught my arm. "Until this storm's over, we couldn't track them with bloodhounds."

An image of Ransom staggering through the canyon slowly dying from exposure flashed in my mind. Years ago, Papa and I came across the body of an old woman curled up like a tattered caterpillar, half buried in a drift beside the road. Her skin was musky blue, agony forever etched in her rigid features.

"You don't give a damn if Ransom—if they freeze to death, do you?" I tore away the scarf muffling my voice. "No, no, *you're* safe. That's all that matters."

For a moment, I thought he was going to slap me. His voice trembled when he said, no louder than a whisper, "Dick Curtis is the best friend I've ever had. If there was any chance of finding him, I wouldn't be here now."

He turned away, yanked off his mittens, and jammed a hand into his pocket. A lucifer scratched the cavern's wall, an amber flare bursting from its tip.

"Garrett, I'm sorry. I didn't mean . . ."

"I know," he said, with a weary sigh. "I'm scared too, gal. We just got different ways of showing it."

Holding the cowering flame in front of him, he edged into our shelter's dark recesses. "No bears lurking in the shadows."

The tiny light streaked to the floor. He struck another. "Don't see anything we can burn, either."

I stared out the arched opening, searching for our partners' blurry forms, hoping to hear Stoophy's honking bray. Garrett's grim expression wasn't entirely due to their disappearance. Without food, blankets, or firewood, we weren't much better off than they were.

Garrett walked up behind me. He cleared his throat. "Remember at Lillith's when I warned you that traveling with the likes of us'd ruin your reputation?"

To say my reputation or its loss was the farthest thing from my mind at that moment would be an understatement. God Almighty, was he about to suggest a fevered tryst in lieu of a fire?

The best response I could manage was a timid "Uh-huh."

"Abigail?" He steered my discomposed self around to face him. "What's the mat—oh, Jaysus, I'm not making, you know . . ."

His stammering reassured me somewhat. "Any sense?"

"Yeah, that, too." Clasping his hands behind him, he rocked on his heels and lectured to the top of my head.

"We'll have to stay the night here. Can't be helped. And, uh, seeing as how there's nothing to build a fire with . . . we'll—well, damn it, to keep warm we're gonna have to sleep close as buckeyes in a pod."

I sucked in my lips, fighting a grin for all I was worth. If it were Ransom here instead of Garrett, I'd be protecting my virtue rather than a man's fragile sense of chivalry.

"Don't fret about it. All I want is to see the sun rise tomorrow and our partners with it."

Garrett nodded, then sat down on the stony floor near the wall. He stretched out, a bent elbow beneath him for a pillow.

I followed suit, spoon fashion. A burly arm snared me around the ribs, snuggling me even tighter to his solid frame. He tucked his knees up inside mine.

The wind heaved and roared outside, dabbling the cave's mouth with a splash of white. I felt completely protected from the storm's wrath. The rhythm of Garrett's breathing was as comforting as a lullaby. I relaxed, my body molding to his warm contours.

He made an odd noise and fidgeted a little. I resettled myself, which prompted another bout of wriggling.

"Can't you get comfortable?" I asked.

A chill draft trickled up my spine. I pressed my hips to Garrett's, denying those icy tendrils. Groaning, he eased backward. Frigid air blasted through the gap. None too gently, I butted my hindquarters to close it.

"Goddamnit, Abigail."

"What? Why are you cussing me?"

"Well, if you can't figure it out, I'm sure as hell not gonna explain it to you. Go to sleep, so's maybe I can."

Pondering his strange behavior eventually brought forth its cause. No doubt there wasn't an inch of me that wasn't blushing.

"For heaven's sake, Garrett!"

He muttered another expletive. "It ain't entirely my fault, you know."

"Oh, blame it all on me, why don't you?"

I scooted away from him a fraction. Conflicting, confusing emotions swirled like the snowflakes frolicking outside on the wind.

"A man can't always hide what he's feeling, Abigail." He eased me to his chest again and held me there. "But I swear I'd never hurt you. That way or any other."

The tenderness in his voice raised a lump in my throat. "The day you feared for my good name, I told you all I needed was a partner and a friend. I'm blessed to have found both of those in you, Garrett."

May. Thursday, 16th, 1861

*Bummed around all day, not doing much
of anything to speak of. Weather
pleasant.*

To paraphrase Papa's oft-used description, snow-
melt splattered onto the cave's floor like a cow
relieving itself on a flat rock. A veritable waterfall
curtained the entrance; the crystalline streams
reflected the brilliant blue sky and glistening
landscape.

Garrett howled when the icy runoff plunged
down his collar as he ducked outside. He paused
to tie my red scarf around a crag's convenient
snout, then waved and disappeared from sight.

I'd been commanded to stay put while he scav-
enged nearby for signs of our still-absent party
members. If they were likewise searching for us,
the scarf would signal our location.

Such uncustomary privacy allowed personal

indulgences I normally walked a half mile to accomplish. Problem was, after dispensing with them, my fascination with watching Mother Nature shed her newest winter coat diminished rapidly.

My thoughts turned to Ransom and it occurred to me how impatiently I awaited his return. The resolute belief that he would brought to mind Veradis Uzgarod, a gypsy fortune-teller Papa was once smitten with.

Few of Veradis's heavily accented philosophies took root between my bored, youthful ears. I was intrigued, however, when she spoke of the heart's perceptive powers; that sadly, intuitions of a loved one in danger or dying often proved correct.

I'd felt no such qualms and surely would have if Ransom were in dire straits. I simply hoped he and Dick would be found soon, along with the mules laden with the grub my belly was sorely in need of.

Not long afterward, a string of blistering curses drifted into the cave. Scrambling to my feet, I rushed to the opening. Dick was prostrate in the snow with Stoophy regarding him smugly, as only a mule can do. Garrett and Ransom were chuckling. Remus was observing the entire scene with bored stoicism.

"Welcome home!" I called.

"Hmmph," Dick snorted, brushing snow from his coat and trousers. "Well, I reckon it's nearer one than them sticker bushes we holed up in last night."

Ransom spun around on his heels. His grin collapsed into an expression of relief mixed with fatigue and, strangely, a trace of fear. He climbed toward me, the others following closely behind.

They crowded inside, the odor of stale sweat permeating our meager quarters. That briny aroma smelled sweeter to me than rosewater perfume. "Lawsy, am I glad to see you two!"

"Dick and Ransom or the mules?" Garrett teased. "I'm so close to starved, a stack of Dick's burnt flapjacks sounds mighty good."

Ransom stood stiff as a soldier, oblivious to the high-spirited reunion. Staring as if I were a stranger, he said, "When I lost sight of you, I was terrified you'd wandered off alone." He glanced at Garrett. "I should have known that wasn't the case."

I was totally perplexed. Before I could frame a response, he turned to the others. "I want to talk to Abigail alone, if you please. It won't take long."

"So take your parley out—" Garrett paused, then shrugged. "C'mon, Dick. The mules have gotta be unpacked anyhow."

"Why, I'd be dee-lighted to oblige. Reckon my butt'd be in danger of thawin' if I lollygagged in here more'n five minutes."

They were scarcely out of earshot when Ransom reached out to me. Infuriated by his rudeness, I didn't budge. His arms dropped to his sides.

"I understand you and Garrett spent the night in here together."

"That's correct."

"Did he— Were you compromised?"

I almost laughed at the absurdity of his question. "Garrett Collingsworth saved my life, you fool," I answered through clenched teeth. "How dare you even ask such a thing."

He paced the floor, talking as much to himself as me. "A ripe peach, he called you. God, how that sickened me. I promised myself I'd protect you from his vile clutches and I've tried, but falling in love with you has complicated that pledge a hundredfold."

I retreated a step, my head waggling side to side. He was rambling like a lunatic. Had battling the elements unhinged his mind?

"Calm yourself," I replied softly. "Garrett was a perfect gentleman—"

"Yes, of course he was. He's playing your heart like a violin. He's a maestro at that. Think, Abigail. *Think!*"

His mittens hurtled through space and slapped the rock wall. One by one, Ransom ticked indictments off on his fingers.

"At the Blue River, who told you to change sides and lead Stoophy by the halter? The animal despises that hold and Garrett knew it. When the inevitable happened, *I* was about to jump onto that log. He grabbed me and shoved me away.

"Then, I tried to stop your hero from undressing you and got knocked senseless. What pleasures he took while we were both unconscious turns my stomach."

I slumped bonelessly against the cave's curving side. The impact of his accusations set my mind reeling. Was Ransom insane? Or could I have completely misjudged Garrett?

"That episode at the gulch? Ask yourself, why did Garrett choose me to measure the claims? He'd never missed a chance to make me look incompetent, but suddenly presented me with a plum? Except he didn't tell me squat about what it meant should I find any tools lying about—an oversight that damn near got me shot."

I clapped my hands over my ears to muffle the vicious torrent. "Why? Why would Garrett do any of that? It doesn't make sense."

Ransom knelt in front of me, his eyes swollen from strain and lack of sleep. "Garrett assembled this company very carefully. I'm a threat to what he wants most: you and his plan to keep any gold we find for himself.

"Dick's the mining expert he summoned to locate the lode. Your father and I were to be Garrett's greenhorn workhorses. When the claim paid, no doubt three fatal accidents would've made Mr. Collingsworth its sole owner."

"That's crazy—"

"Hear me out, Abigail, *please*. Your appearance was an unexpected bonus. A woman strong enough to prospect and a beautiful, desirable bed-warmer combined."

I was shaking, my stomach burning and knotted so painfully I'd have vomited had it not been empty. "No, no, Garrett's my friend—"

"Is he? Answer me this. When you first met with Garrett, didn't you have to plead with him to let you join up with us?"

"I— Well, yes. I didn't have any money. Nowhere else to go."

"And as upset as you were by your father's death, you never suspected that his reluctance was all an act."

Waving my arms in front of me, I cried, "It couldn't have—"

"Darlin', I wasn't *there* that day. How would I know that unless Garrett told me later? Oh, he laughed about it, saying he was your knight in shining armor. That he'd bide his time before . . ."

Ransom looked down and lowered his voice. "Christ, there's no reason to hold anything back. Garrett said he'd wait as long as he could because . . . a woman's only a virgin once."

I was lightheaded from trying to sort memories and perceptions and weighing them against Ransom's accusations. I couldn't deny that Papa's death had rocked me to the core, left me frightened and desperate.

From the beginning, I'd trusted Garrett because my father had. I'd never once considered that all Papa'd known of him was contained in a few letters they'd exchanged.

Over the last weeks, I'd learned quite a lot of Ransom's history. I knew Dick hailed from Iowa, was one of eight children, and once owned a mercantile. I'd probably shared more childhood adventures with all of them than they'd cared to hear, yet Garrett's past remained as much a mystery as the day we'd met.

"By your expression, I assume you're beginning to believe me."

"Yes . . . no—I don't know. It's just so hard to believe Garrett being the kind of man who—"

"Who allows his sister, his own flesh and blood, to sell herself to anyone with a dollar in his pocket? If I had a sister, I'd see—"

"What do you mean, if? I thought you had three."

He regarded me sternly. "I do, and genteel ladies all. As I started to say, if I had a sister of such low moral turpitude, I'd see her in a convent—see her dead—before I'd allow her to debase herself for money."

I felt hollow, betrayed, bereft. "Oh, Ransom, why didn't you tell me this before?"

He gathered me in his arms. "Because I love you and didn't want to hurt you. Because you wouldn't have believed me until I had enough evidence of Garrett's duplicity." Sighing deeply, he added, "And because until last night, I thought I could protect you from him."

"Nothing happened. I swear to you, it didn't."

"Nor will it, unless Garrett succeeds in dispatching me."

He cupped my face in his hands. "Promise you'll stay as far away from him as possible. And whatever happens in the future, give *me* the benefit of the doubt, not Garrett."

"I—I will," I answered meekly.

"With us two against his one, everything'll be all right, darlin'," he assured. "We'll reap the benefits of this expedition while avoiding whatever Garrett might have in store."

There was a numbed emptiness inside me that no amount of victuals could fill. Ransom gazed at me lovingly, but I'm sure my eyes were as fixed and dull as a dead man's.

Many hours of daylight remained of this day, but all I wanted was to crawl into a bedroll and pull the blanket over my buzzing head. I felt drained and beaten, as if I'd been flogged with a buggy whip.

May. Wednesday, 22nd, 1861

*Stayed in a cabin where six men lived—
the cabin is 10 × 12. A man by the
name of Davis shot a man by the name of
Rowland. Pleasant, much wind.*

Upon restarting our journey, we encountered
another wayfaring pilgrim. Though rendered
stoop-shouldered by his cumbersome pack, the
man approached us quickly. As he neared, he
tossed a hearty wave as if we were kinfolk just
arriving by train rather than scruffy strangers
who'd just clambered over a mountain's summit.

"It's a grand day to be alive, eh, brothers?"
he hollered.

The sister in our company wasn't entirely
pleased at being ignored. Perhaps whether a
shotgun was aimed at my head or not somewhat
influenced my attitude toward such misidentifi-
cations.

"Guess so, if you're partial to getting your ass blowed from here to yonder," Dick shouted back.

A half week's rest at the cave had left the Forty-Niner tetchier than usual. We two-legged pilgrims had recuperated from the blizzard's ordeal with a couple of meals behind our belts, but Stoophy and Remus went far too long without ample food, water, and relief from the weight they'd carried to recover that rapidly.

During our forced encampment, if Dick muttered "Ain't seen folks so snarly since Curly Sue Divine showed up at the Mount Olivet Free Will Baptist Church's get-acquainted picnic," he'd muttered it a hundred times.

His colorful observation surely defined but did not ease the general gloominess and frayed nerves Ransom, Garrett, and I operated under for the duration.

Spending the last two days wading drifts up to my thighs wasn't pleasant, but it was a vast improvement over pondering Ransom's litany, mending rents in our clothing, and studying Garrett for signs of diabolic intent.

I took refuge behind the mules from the dratted, skin-scorching wind as the strapping, stovepipe-hatted wanderer shook hands with my partners. Squinting when he neared me, he said, "Why, there's an angel in our midst."

He doffed his crumpled chapeau, releasing a

thatch of graying hair that hadn't felt a barber's shears in months. "A rare and breathtaking sight, to be sure."

"This is Father Dyer, Abigail," Garrett informed. "Besides Phil the Cannibal, he's the most famous character in the territory."

"Is that so?" I replied, reversing myself a step or two.

Garrett chuckled. "He's a preacher, gal. Circuits five hundred miles on foot reading the good book to anyone who'll listen and, I reckon, a fair number who don't."

"Yea, the harvest truly is plenteous, but the laborers are few," Dyer recited, his eyes twinkling merrily. "Matthew, nine thirty-seven."

Irreverent as it might be, long association with the bogus man of the cloth who begat me had created a healthy cynicism for anyone with scriptural passages to fit any occasion. In my experience, true believers spoke from the heart rather than from memory.

Father Dyer's evident sense of wonder and inner joy, however, contradicted that notion. I took an immediate liking to the devoted missionary whose ragtag attire appeared to have been salvaged from Lewis and Clark's haversacks.

"Where are you bound for, lambs, and are you faring well in your travels?"

"No place particular," Dick drawled. "And

we've gotta trade for some grub afore we head there."

Dyer laughed and tapped his scuffed, leather-bound Bible. "Discover not a secret to another, eh? A Proverb held dear by prospectors to be sure. As for supplies, Jarrod Davis keeps a well-stocked larder. His cabin's about five miles south—the nearest you'll find occupied."

"I say we pay a call on Mr. Davis," Ransom declared. "We can't live on pale coffee and flap-jacks forever."

Garrett nodded. "Only diehards pass the winter on their claims. Most clear the pantry and light out for Denver City until bad weather's past."

"If'n he won't barter for a mule, we'll be stray-ing four miles outta the way for nothing," Dick hedged. "That's all we got to offer him 'cept our good looks."

I jerked a thumb toward Stoophy. "A half pound of bacon would be a better than even swap for that beast."

"Now, listen here, missy angel. I'd sooner trade you to a bunch of renegade Injuns than part with that speckled Beelzebub. Remus ain't half the packer Stoophy is. Ain't got no personal-ity, besides."

"Yes, well, when you arrive, remind Mr. Davis that the Lord blesses a cheerful giver," Dyer said, preventing me from remarking further on Stoophy's abundantly abysmal personality. "And tell him I'll visit Friday, latest."

"Why not go with us now?" I asked.

"Lo, there's others more sorely in need of God's word. We'll meet again, child in this world or the next." He raised a hand in benediction. "God bless and keep you all."

Garrett tipped his hat. "The steps of a good man are ordered by the Lord; and He delighteth in his way. Psalms thirty-seven, twenty-three."

"An excellent fare-thee-well, Brother Collingsworth, and amen to it." Dyer set off at a pace we lesser, younger mortals would have the devil's own time matching.

"Pretty good ol' boy for a holy Joe," Dick said. "He didn't condemn, try to convert, nor pass the plate like most I've met."

"When he bends a knee tonight, he'll put a good word in for us, though," Garrett replied. "The flock Dyer tends is a mite scattered, but it must be quite a list he says grace over."

Veering due south, we plowed a switchback path across steep terrain. Other than animal tracks preserved in its crust, the snow lay as pristinely undisturbed as when it had fallen. At this altitude, constant wind twisted tree trunks into bizarrely beautiful living sculptures.

A dignified bighorn ram watched us warily

from atop a massive table rock. The jutted ridge above his eyes, heavy, curled horns, and white snout seemed strangely similar to lithographs of Viking warriors I'd pored over in Papa's history books.

Grazing below his aerie, the herds' white bellies and rumps blended into the snow. Their dark brown torsos, legs, and head created a disproportionate and two-dimensional contrast.

Skittish by nature and protective of the many lambs scampering near their mothers, the ram issued a bleated command and guided his charges away from us.

They bounded over boulders with scant effort, leaving me questioning my prowess as a hunter. I could have easily felled three hundred pounds of fresh mutton, yet hadn't given my rifle a thought when all those dinners-on-the-hoof were in sight.

I surely regretted my soft heart when all our midday meal consisted of was greasy flapjacks left from breakfast and snow melted in our tin cups over candle stubs to wash them down.

Lacking Father Dyer's ebullience, we'd again fallen silent, but it was more a restful contentedness than the tense avoidance of past days. Even Ransom and Garrett seemed to have declared a truce.

That afternoon, from my elevated vantage

point, I saw smoke curling above the gradually thickening treetops hours before the sod chimney spewing it skyward came into view.

Obviously, the missionary's five-mile estimate had been of the as-the-crow-flies persuasion. Due to the pitched grade and our lack of wings, we'd probably come twice that distance.

A moat of stumps surrounding the cabin itself showed how far its builders had been willing to travel for construction materials. Judging by the milled-lumber sluice that rambled for at least twenty rods up an adjacent hillside, first-rate mining equipment was more important to this operation than creature comforts.

Garrett cupped his hands around his mouth and shouted, "Hallo the house."

A rifle barrel preceded an enormous bald Negro out the door. The weapon looked like a toy cradled in the colored Goliath's huge hands.

"State your bizness, gents."

"Are you Jarrod Davis?" Garrett asked.

"That's *my* bizness, stranger. I'm still waitin' to hear your'n."

"We're getting low on supplies. Father Dyer thought Davis might have stores to trade."

The rifle lowered a fraction. "That all Dyer said?"

Garrett crossed his arms and shifted his

weight in frustration. "We didn't exactly retire to the parlor for brandy and cigars, bub—"

"He said to tell Mr. Davis he'd visit tomorrow or Friday," I blurted.

"That's what I wanted to . . ." The man peered into the dusk. A gold tooth glinted in the light spilling out behind him. "Say, is you just a tall shaver or a real live girl?"

I couldn't resist chuckling at his awestruck tone. "I reckon that's my bizness, stranger."

His booming laugh drowned out my partners' moans. "Hee-hee, if you ain't a caution, teasin' ol' Humphrey thataway. Ya'll come in and makes yourselves to home."

Though not much larger than the cave we'd recently abandoned, lanterns bathed the cabin's gloriously warm interior with a cheery glow.

I inventoried the tools, boots, weapons, and sundries dangling artfully from antlered racks and pegs secured to the log walls and rafters. Neatly made triple-decked bunks elled in one corner; open cupboards bordered both sides of the fireplace.

Beside the hearth, an elfin man with a flowing red mustache and a jaunty eyepatch rose from a spindle-backed rocker.

As he boldly scrutinized my person, Humphrey proclaimed, "This is Mr. Jarrod Peabody Armstrong Davis," in a manner implying the name should mean something besides an indication that several branches of Davis's family tree had been placated in one fell swoop.

"Never has my humble home been graced by such loveliness." Davis's flat, nasal twang brought with it images of sailing ships and clam chowder.

Dick stage-whispered, "I don't reckon he means us, eh, boys?"

In case the remark had been overheard and underappreciated, I quickly introduced myself and my partners. Davis encouraged us to shed our heavy gear and take seats at the puncheon table.

Before our hindquarters found solid purchase on the benches, Humphrey placed steaming mugs of tea between our elbows.

"Sugar, Miss Fiske?" he asked, balancing a heaping spoonful of the precious crystals above its bowl.

I hadn't tasted sweetening for weeks, so I know my eyes were as round as pie tins when I gasped, "Oh, yes, please." Mesmerized, I watched the white stream flow into my cup. I licked my lips in anticipation.

"Like I told your man out—" Garrett started.

"Humphrey is not a slave, Mr. Collingsworth. He's as free as you and me."

"Uh, sorry. As I was saying, we're looking to

trade a mule for supplies. We had to hole up in a cave for several days and didn't have much else to do besides eat."

"A camp this size can always use more livestock, but gold dust is the more common medium of exchange."

Dick snorted. "If'n we had any, we damn sure wouldn't be bartering with a pack animal, now, would we?"

While the negotiations commenced, I studied Davis from under my lashes whenever his good eye didn't avert toward me. Playing peek-a-boo was childish, to be sure, but it lent a great deal of credence to one of Papa's more profane axioms: "I've seen many a big brute finish a brawl, but never seen one start it. It's always some cocky-tempered, sawed-off son of a bitch that throws the first punch."

Ten minutes' acquaintanceship had already shown Davis to be as arrogant as a barnyard's lone rooster. His sardonic smile and haughty drone during the intentionally extended haggling irritated me enormously.

It was difficult to keep my mouth shut and let the men hash out the terms, but I persevered, rewarding my uncustomary restraint by dumping two spoonfuls of short-sweetening into additional servings of fragrant orange pekoe.

"Alas, we have talked the sun down," Davis

said after a bargain was finally struck. "Fortunately, my associates have not returned from Denver City, so I have plenty of room for guests."

Garrett raised a hand. "We appreciate the offer, but the moon's bright enough to get in some night traveling."

"Nonsense," our host countered, chuckling scornfully. "My good man, only a fool would deny himself venison stew, a warm bunk, and a roof for the rigors of the trail."

I'd have agreed heartily had he not turned to me and added, "While your friends digest Humphrey's excellent cooking, I'll have an opportunity for a nice chat with you, Miss Fiske."

We more surrendered to than accepted Davis's hospitality. Thankfully, a delicious supper including baking soda biscuits dripping with butter and dried apple pie more than made up for our host's inane drivel. Standing beside the fire gobbling his meal, the chef positively beamed at our compliments.

Later, I wasn't surprised when our chat consisted primarily of listening to Davis's conquest of the worlds of education, finance, commerce, and of late, mining.

My only source of amusement was watching his expression flit from shock to horror to disdain as I described my checkered past, including the fact I'd never crossed a schoolhouse's threshold in my life.

"I say," he stammered, "you speak unusually well for an illiterate."

"Is that so?" Rising from the bench, I knuckled the table. "Then I reckon I quote Socrates, Shakespeare, and Chaucer, do long division, addition, subtraction, and read Latin unusually well for an illiterate, too, Mr. Davis. Good night, Mr. Davis."

Ransom's murmured "That's my girl" from the bunk angled beside mine and Humphrey's ebony fingers trimming the lanterns were my last memories before sleep embraced me. Little did I know its gentle grasp would not last until morning.

Some hours later, steel traps clattered to the plank floor when the cabin door slammed into their pegs.

Humphrey scrambled to his knees on his pallet in front of the hearth; his rifle barrel gleaming blue in the dim light. "Hold it right there!"

"Shit fire, Humphrey," a man shouted. "It's Rowland. And Yates, Slocum, and McKnight."

Davis leaped from an upper bunk and stomped across the room in socked feet. "How dare you burst in here like cutthroats in the middle of the night."

Four men, almost identical in size and level of intoxication, lurched inside. Davis banged the door shut behind them. "I should sack all four of you—or let Humphrey save me the trouble."

The quartet divested themselves of ice-caked coats, fur hats, and mittens, dropping them in a heap on the floor. They started toward the table.

"You ain't leavin' that soggy mess there, gents," Humphrey cautioned.

"Oh, yeah? Try and stop us, nigger."

Davis appeared thunderstruck. "Rowland! What in God's name has gotten into you?"

"Show 'im, Yates."

"Turn up the goddamned lamp so's I can."

As Rowland complied, Yates pulled a creased newspaper from his pocket. "This here's the *New York Times* dated, uh, April the fifteenth."

Rattling it open dramatically, he squinted at the front page and read, "Fort Sumter fallen. Major Anderson has surrendered, after hard fighting commencing at four o'clock yesterday morning and continuing until five minutes to one to-day. The American flag has given place to the Palmette of South Carolina."

"War," Davis groaned, crumpling onto a bench. "I prayed it wouldn't come to this. War between the states."

I twisted around to peek at Ransom. Expecting

to see a stunned expression mirroring my own, he seemed to be smiling. He raised his head and laid his hand atop mine. "That was well over a month ago. President Lincoln has surely quashed the rebellion by now."

As if he'd overheard, Davis all but echoed Ransom's sentiment.

"Not hardly, Yank," Rowland sneered. "When we left Denver City, the Stars and Bars was snappin' real pert from the flagpole outside Wallingford and Murphy's store."

"Yeah, and last we heard, five thousand troops outta God bless Virginny's on their way to call on Ol' Abe, personal," Yates added. "Ain't that right, Slocum?"

Since the other men, presumably Slocum and McKnight, were slumped over the table snoring, it was Rowland who roared, "You're goddamn right, that's right."

Davis wiped a sleeve across his pallid brow. "How can you be jubilant when our country is being torn apart? Sympathy for the Southern cause is one thing. Celebrating a divided union is unthinkable—it's treasonous."

Rowland's face reddened with anger. "Treason, my ass. It's you nigger-lovin' abolitionists that started it, speechifyin' about how darkies are the same as whites—"

"That's quite enough," Davis growled, rising to

his feet. He eased backward with such deliberation, he seemed not to move at all.

"Yep, now *you're* right, Yankee Doodle. Me and the boys has taken plenty enough orders from you and that woolly buck."

Yates whirled, yanking a pistol from under his shirt. "Don't even blink, nigger." At the same instant, a long-bladed knife flashed in Rowland's fist. "We're fixin' to have our own little Sumter, raht chere, boss," he snarled, advancing unsteadily on his employer.

In one fluid motion, Davis grabbed a Dragoon from its wall pegs, cocked, and fired.

Rowland's mouth gaped. The knife fell, its point transfixed in the planks. A crimson stain spread across his belly. His legs folded at the knees.

"Rowland!" Yates bellowed over his shoulder. Humphrey whipped the rifle barrel under Yates's gun hand. Before his revolver thudded to the floor, Humphrey'd rammed the rifle butt square at the bridge of Yates's nose.

The dead and the grievously wounded lay sprawled within inches of each other. Their two cohorts, roused from a drunken stupor by the clamor, stared bug-eyed at Davis. Very carefully, their hands raised in silent surrender.

A huge pair of boots eased down from the bunk above me, followed by Garrett's husky torso. From his loftier perch, Dick's lean frame landed beside him.

Garrett bent double to issue a blunt, "Let's git."

Neither Ransom nor I needed to be told twice.

June. Saturday, 1st, 1861

*Tired to death, almost twenty miles today
and fifty pound packs. Pleasant and
warm.*

When Papa presented me with this olive-green
leather-bound journal, its stiff, ruled leaves
crackled fresh and new and replete with the lus-
cious aroma of ink and pulped wood.

I promised I'd duly record each day's adventures for a mile-by-mile account of our road to
riches. Secretly, I hoped to publish it someday
to inspire women who wanted more from life
than a church wedding, a baby every year, and
a well-attended funeral—a concept that all but
guaranteed its classification as fiction.

I couldn't have known when that pledge was
made how regularly life would interfere with lit-
erary intentions. It saddens me that the account
already contains gaps due to frequent interludes

when absolutely nothing happened worthy of immortalizing in pencil lead.

At the outset, I didn't anticipate how often descriptions of beastly weather, partaking of food unfit for human consumption, breaking camp, making camp, and exhaustion would fill the page had I recorded them with the same monotony as which they were endured.

The week following the murder serves as a shining example.

Though Rowland's death was a clear case of self-defense, upon our imminent departure from the scene, Jarrod Davis increased the quantity of trade goods to the extent that even the stalwart Stoophy couldn't carry it all. Davis's guilty conscience resulted in each member of our company being outfitted with a fifty-pound pack in which to lug that largesse.

I'm sure Dick assembled a much lighter load for me to bear, but nevertheless, the first day out, I developed a keen sympathy for Stoophy's lot in life. On this, my eighth of encumberment, I envied the rebellious Rowland his more instantaneous demise.

Just hours ago, I beckoned to Garrett during a rest break. "How far have we come since we left Davis's cabin?"

"Oh, sixty miles. Maybe sixty-five."

I curled my lips into a demure smile, then

asked sweetly, "Do either you or Dick have the slightest idea where we are or where we're going? Or are you awaiting some kind of Divine Intervention?"

With one foot planted on the log where I sat, he surveyed the valley spreading before us like the velvety chartreuse folds of a lady's skirt. "Yes, ma'am. We're south of Trout Creek Pass. With spring busting loose here and flaunting her colors, this is the prettiest piece of real estate on God's green earth."

He pointed slightly to his right. "Can't see it from here, but the mighty Arkansas River wraps around this district—South Park, it's called. We must be a good four thousand feet lower than we were at Davis's. Can't you tell? Every mile, the air's warmer and it's easier to breathe."

"I thought you and Dick believed the pickings were better in the high country. Don't tell me we've climbed a thousand blessed mountains just for the exercise."

"Not a-tall," he said, scratching his beard as if deep in thought—or lousy. "War's changed things considerably."

I groaned, fearing more of the same oratory I'd heard around the campfire for over a week. If I lived as long as Methuselah, I'd never understand why men spend countless hours discussing the various means by which it is possible to exterminate each other, and their irrefutable reasons for doing so.

"Me and Dick'd been wondering why the territory seemed nigh deserted. Best we can figure, any number of go-backs pitched their tools and headed for the States to enlist."

I waited several patient seconds for a further explanation, then prompted, "What, may I ask, does their eagerness to travel two thousand miles to become cannon fodder have to do with us?"

"Cannon fodder?" he repeated, chuckling derisively. "Your patriotism is right heartwarmin', gal." Wisely, he continued, "Just because a claim's been staked and worked doesn't mean it belongs to the owner 'til doomsday. South Park paid before, then jackrabbit-quick was crawlin' with wanna-be millionaires. War's made Rocky Mountain yellow fever give way to boilin' blood. We aim to take advantage of it."

I suppose my expression remained somewhat skeptical, for the skin webbed at the corners of his eyes as he grinned. "What's the matter, Abigail? Don't you trust me?"

"No," I blurted, instantly wishing I hadn't.

Garrett's face darkened like a cloud shadow skimming the ground. "You really don't, do you?"

Out of nowhere, Ransom loomed at my side. "Goodness, what dour frowns you two are wearing. It's too beautiful a day for such a serious discussion."

Garrett glared at him, turned on his heel, and strode away toward where Stoophy was tethered.

"Are you all right, darlin'?"

"Of course I am. Garrett didn't bare his fangs once."

Ransom eased down next to me, looking as mournful as a beagle hound. I smiled an apology and patted his hand.

"Don't mind me. I'm just stiff, sore, and was born mean."

Turning his hand over to clasp mine, he said, "Let's take a walk. Without that pack banging your spine, it'll work out the kinks, I promise."

I assumed he had some knowledge of the rigors of femininity, but modesty precluded telling him that my achiness and general malaise was not entirely due to the weight I carried. Instead, I stretched to my feet, took his arm, and persevered.

The fragrant, sun-basked pines bordering the clearing rattled with frolicking squirrels. Birds shopping for summer homes glided and swooped overhead. Snow clotted stubbornly in the trees' elbowed branches, but the land's resurrection was well under way.

"Have you ever regretted something you've done?" Ransom asked.

I laughed. "Far more often than I'll admit."

"No, I don't mean something impetuous— something you mulled beforehand, decided to commit yourself to, and still lived to regret."

My heart shrank ever so slightly. I'd come to care very much for that fair-haired dreamer. Had he decided that his love for me was only infatuation? "I have, I'm sure, except . . . You may not understand this, but I've felt more regret when I didn't do something and wound up wishing I had after it was too late."

He didn't answer, so I bumbled on. "It's occurred to me that it doesn't take courage to line a boardwalk and watch the parade pass by. But riding astride the elephant or juggling twice as many balls as you have hands to catch them? From moment to moment, it's even odds that you'll either make a hero or a fool of yourself."

Ransom stopped midstride and took me in his arms. As we held each other, I listened to how his heart's rhythmic beat matched my own.

Like a gentle rain, the most wondrous sense of peace washed over me. Whether it was meant to last or drifted away leaving only its memory behind, once again, I felt as if I *belonged*.

"I love you," he whispered.

For the first time, I answered, "And I love you."

Turning my face to his, I slid my fingers behind his neck, raised on my tiptoes, and kissed him. Our lips parted, tongues darting hesitantly, then again and again in sensuous, passionate abandon.

"I want you, Abigail," he breathed, pressing, grinding into me.

"Oh, God. No . . . I *can't* . . ."

He cupped my breast and I shuddered at his touch, all but succumbing to desire. "Ransom, please—stop."

Burying his face in my neck, he murmured, "Don't be afraid. I'll—"

"That isn't—damn it, I truly *can't*." Struggling from his embrace, I looked up at him, trying to express what propriety refused to let me say aloud. Other than mothers and daughters, and rarely at that, women didn't discuss such things even among themselves. In theory, I was a liberal thinker. In practice, I stood mute as an oak stump.

Ransom's eyes searched mine. "Don't cry," he whispered as gentle fingers brushed beneath my damp lashes. "There'll be another time for us."

Arm in arm, we rambled through the pine thicket. I stared ahead, thoughts tumbling in my mind like marbles in a bag. So befogged, I didn't notice that our packs were all that remained in the clearing until we were almost upon them.

Perplexed, I scanned the verdant hillside.

Stoophy and our two partners appeared a mile or more ahead, angling south-southeast.

"Kind of them to give a shout when they were ready to push on," Ransom said sarcastically.

Shrugging into my pack, I thought, Garrett knows. He must have come looking for us and seen . . .

I felt strangely disconcerted—not ashamed, exactly, for I'd done nothing to be ashamed of. Yet, what Garrett thought of the scene he'd surely witnessed bothered me enormously because, I suddenly realized, what he thought of me mattered a great deal.

June. Monday, 3rd, 1861

*We left camp at about 1/2 past 9 o'clock
and went down about 20 miles, then we
turned south and stopped on a gulch.
Mosquitoes and horseflies awfull. A
person passing would hardly think what a
bloody deed had been perpetrated here
two years ago. Nothing but the bleached
bones of the men and horses. Clear
and pleasant.*

No man-made cathedral, even the ancient European monoliths I'd seen portrayed in vivid oil paintings, compared with the sandstone palisades rising from the canyon floor.

My partners neither recognized nor cared that some of those stern, scarred faces, pocked and ridged by glaciers a millennia ago, resembled an Indian warrior's profile or a medieval beast poised in an eternal crouch.

If the men had ever laid on their backs in cool grass watching cloud dragons battle across the sky, like knee pants and bowed cravats, they'd outgrown that kind of foolishness long ago.

The magnificence and somber holiness of the canyon was marred considerably, however, by swarms of flies and mosquitoes swirling around me like a black, whining blizzard.

I didn't know whether the fiends hibernated or not, but by whatever fashion they resurrected themselves, how they accomplished it so quickly and abundantly was a mystery.

There is supposedly a reason behind every creature's existence, but other than keeping mankind forever humble, I couldn't guess what purpose the good Lord had in mind when He designed those insidious pests.

Ransom fell in beside me, a triangled bandanna tied over his nose and mouth like a bandit. I raised my hands and cried, "Take everything I've got, just please don't shoot."

"Everything?" His eyes glittered like twin mountain lakes against his windburned skin. "Promises, promises."

I slapped him lightly on the arm. "For heaven's sake, don't you ever think about anything else?"

"Now and then I think about how much fun it's going to be spoiling you rotten. Call it gold fever, but there's a fortune awaiting us ahead. I can smell it."

"Uh-huh. The only whiffs I'm catching are coming from four filthy human beings and a flatulent, mangy mule."

Tired of swatting insects that seemed not a bit fearful of my flailing hands, I pulled my neckerchief from my back pocket and followed Ransom's example. The cloth was stiff with sweat and, well, other grime I refused to think about since its application immediately made breathing a much more pleasant pastime.

"Are you getting discouraged?" he asked, a note of concern in his voice.

"A little, I suppose. Garrett and Dick are, too."

"What makes you think so? They certainly appeared to be in good spirits, both in attitude and the liquid kind, last night."

I pondered a moment, unsure whether to cast a pall over Ransom's cheerfulness. Laughter can be as contagious as smallpox, but melancholy and its devastating effect spread just as easily.

Yet, I was not his mother and therefore not duty-bound to protect him from life's vexations. "Despite the Forty-rod they spiked their coffee with, they must have had trouble sleeping, the same as I did. They sat up late, talking about how we must find a paying claim soon or give it up."

"Why? We've got supplies enough to last awhile, and what of that character, Emmanuel Trentham, we ran across last week? Why, he was ablaze with news about big strikes in Tarryall, Fairplay—I can't recall all the camps he said have sprung up overnight."

I gazed at the groves of cottonwoods shading a tiny rill that flowed along the canyon's west wall. Garrett had mentioned Trentham's glowing reports, too. Dick countered resignedly that in every boomtown he'd ever passed through, more gold dust found its way into the pockets of tradespeople than stayed in the prospectors' pokes.

"This gal in Californee," he'd slurred. "Ugliest brute God ever put mammaries on, but she baked pies so sweet they made your teeth hurt just thinking about them. Betwixt March and May Day alone, that she-ox peddled eighteen thousand dollars worth of them sumbitches."

I chuckled and Ransom smiled down at me. "Ah, that's more like it, darlin'. We've got as good a chance to find paydirt as those other jaspers. Right?"

Crossing my fingers behind my back both for luck and to forgive a white lie, I nodded and said, "You betcha."

As we'd talked, the terrain had become more barren and rocky. The canyon's walls crowded closer, blocking all but a wedge of sunlight. Gooseflesh rippled my arms as deep shadow dropped the temperature ten degrees or more.

Beside a spindly piñon, Garrett was holding Stoophy's halter while Dick patted down the animal's front leg. I thought it quite brave when the mule's owner lifted the appendage and probed the tip of his knife in its hoof's center cleft.

Stoophy's ears flattened ominously, but the beast stood docile as a tame doe while Dick pried out a robin's-egg-sized cobble.

The mule crawfished a few steps, favoring the sore foot, then settled down, presumably, to plot when, where, and how viciously it would repay Dick's kindness.

"Do you think he's sound?" Garrett asked.

Dick cocked his head skeptically. "That hoof's kinda tender. Wouldn't worry so much if he wasn't still packin' a couple hundred pounds."

Like a retriever at point, Garrett stared intently southward. His angular features set hard and grim. I wondered if our adventure had aged me a decade as it had him. Mountain streams' undulating reflections hadn't revealed many truths of that nature.

"Our late start and an early camp makes for a damn short day," Garrett muttered. "We can't risk laming that mule, though."

"I could scout ahead and see how much farther the canyon runs," Ransom volunteered.

"Nah. We'll lose the light soon enough anyhow. Rustle us up some wood instead. I don't know about you all, but I could sure use a cup of coffee."

I'll just bet you could, I thought. Last night's corned brew is still percolating right sharp in your head, isn't it?

Dick unloaded Stoophy, who commenced rolling in the dirt like an enormous speckled pup. I sneezed and tasted bitter grit, but forgave the beast his creature comfort. Had I been so burdened and fly-bitten, I'd have demanded a nice backscratch, too.

A heap of dry scrub and driftwood made a jolly fire. I set Garrett's coffee to boiling while Dick fashioned a fatback poultice for Stoophy's stone bruise.

Rummaging around in our stores as if I'd find something to fix for supper besides beans and bacon, my heart leaped and almost strangled me when a voice boomed down from the ridge, "If you'uns know what's good for ya, ya'll *git*."

A half dozen men on horseback picketed the bluff. I heard Garrett's rifle cock. He stepped out into the middle of the draw. "And what if we don't?"

"Whoa, now, friend," answered a short man

astride a dappled gray. He raised his hands to show he wasn't armed. "Didn't mean that threatenin'-like."

"Sure as hell sounded that way," Ransom murmured from behind me. I felt the solid contours of the Sharps press into my spine. Reaching around, my fingers closed around its walnut forestock. He released it, whispering, "I hope this doesn't come in handy."

"Me and the boys ain't out to do you no harm," the visitor added. "Mind if I mosey down and get me a cup of that coffee you got a-cookin'?"

"Don't have enough for a posse," Garrett shot back.

"Aw, my partners ain't fawnchin' to come down there anyhow. I'll venture it alone, if that's agreeable."

"It's a free country."

The man wheeled away from the ridge. Rather than stay in place like sentries as I expected, his band dismounted and casually brush-tethered their horses.

"I don't know what to make of this," Garrett said, not taking his eyes off the intruders. "May be nothing. May be something. Best be ready for anything."

Clattering hooves echoed from the south much sooner than I expected. I brought my rifle around, cradling it waist-high, the barrel pointed away from our visitor's approach. It'd whip into position fast enough if need be.

The grulla and its rider slowed to a walk as they came into sight. Pulling up, the man tipped his bowler, then swung out of the saddle, dropping the reins to the ground.

Hame-jawed and built like a barrel on stilts, he was rigged in his broadcloth Sunday best, trouser legs tucked neatly into calf-tall polished boots.

"Aft'noon, folks," he greeted, as if passing us on a boardwalk. "Sorry if we ruckused yer nerves a mite."

Garrett's expression relaxed somewhat as he regarded the dandified gent. "Can't fault us for being careful."

"Not a-tall, not a-tall. Thieves is thick as chiggers in high grass around here."

He stuck out a hand that'd span C to C on a keyboard without stretching. "Oswald Parsefal Joplin's what Mama writ in the Bible back in '35. It got shaved to Opie afore I got old enough to have to live it down."

I laid the Sharps aside as Garrett dispensed with the formalities. Joplin accepted a lukewarm cup from me, saying slyly, "Who's the lucky man what took you for a bride?"

Ransom's lips parted, but Garrett got the jump

on him. "Me and Abigail hitched up back in Denver City last April."

Silently, I credited him for quick-wittedness worthy of Maximilian R. T. Fiske himself—not to mention his only child. Though Ransom appeared positively homicidal, he held his tongue.

"That's a fine set of catalogue duds you're rigged up in," Dick said suspiciously. "You going to a marrying or a burying?"

Joplin chuckled. "A birthin's more like it. Me and the boys make up Hattiesville's town company. Not to blow my own bugle, mind you, but I'm the mayor and elected recorder."

"Never heard of it," Garrett stated.

"Ain't platted yet. We're takin' care of that bizness this evenin'." He pointed southeast. "She lays nine, maybe ten mile yonder in a slash catawampussed betwixt two monstracious rock piles. No use pullin' your leg, Hattiesville's uglier than a breech-born coonhound, but she's already got ever'thang a man could want: payin' color, a mercantile, three saloons, a whorehouse . . ."

The skin between his bushy burnsides flushed scarlet. "Beg pardon, Missus Collingsworth. I done forgot myself."

Garrett winked at me, then prompted, "Seems you forgot why you warned us to make tracks, too. We're not trespassing on somebody's claim, are we?"

Joplin glanced over his shoulder, shuddering visibly. "No chance of *that*. Far as I know, ain't nobody traipsed through here in more'n two years."

"Why?" I asked. His anxiety was suddenly as pronounced as the veins starbursting his nose.

Joplin sat his cup down on a rock. "Got somethin' to show whilst I'm a-tellin'. Foller me."

Our party exchanged quizzical glances. Garrett shrugged, then motioned for us to join ranks with Hattiesville's portly mayor.

"You won't find it marked as such on no map," he began, "but this canyon, 'specially the tail end of it, is called Butcher's Gulch. If'n we had any young'uns 'round here, Mamas'd threaten 'em with bein' left here to make 'em behave."

He drew a deep breath and plunged on, "Back in August of '59, a big party of Swedes outta Minnesota, twenty-two of 'em matter-of-factly, headed by a man name of Adamek Nordberg, laid claim to this gulch. That bunch drug logs to build cabins, lashed together corrals for their packhorses, all the while hootin' and hollerin' like kids let out for recess. Man, they was nigh giddy to start swingin' picks and weighin' dust.

"A week later, some prospector friends from a nearby camp rambled over to say howdy." Joplin paused, raising his arms like a preacher signaling a congregation to gain their feet. "This is what they found. Ever' one o' them boys was dead. Massa-creed, by the look of it. Horses, too."

I peered beyond his fingertips into the murky shadows. For a hundred yards up both sides of the canyon, the gleaming, bleached bones of men and horses lay jumbled together where they'd fallen.

Animal and human skulls stared vacantly in every direction. Rib, arm, and leg bones were heaped in places, scattered in others. Surveying the carnage, it was all too easy to imagine horses screaming in terror, the mortally wounded begging for help.

"Dear God," I moaned. "Why didn't someone have the decency to bury them?"

"They tried." Joplin hesitated, adding somberly, "By the time they was found, carrion-eaters had been at 'em . . . and maggots. It'd been hotter'n blue blazes for days. Nobody could get the stomach for it."

"Indians?" Ransom asked, his face ashen.

"Thought so at first, 'cept none of 'em was scalped and Injuns prize butter-colored hair most of all. Some folks figger they was ambushed when they rode in from somewhars. But why? Them boys never rankled a soul, the claim weren't never jumped—"

Joplin's eyes widened as big as saucers. He whirled, crouching like an Irish pugilist. "Aw, shee-it, ya hear that?" His face shone with sweat. "Hear that wind a-groanin'? Only place I ever knowed of where it only howls at night. And it never did afore them Swedes got murdered."

He spun, knocked me off balance, and ran like sixty for our camp. Pinwheeling backward, I stumbled over the rocky ground. I fell, skidding butt first, then sprawled against the sloping canyon wall. Moments later, Joplin galloped past on his gray, frantically whipping it with the reins.

Jarred breathless for a moment, the palm of my hand curved around something hard, cold, and smooth. I jerked away, bolting upright in the same movement. Glimpsing the bone-white mound erupting from the dirt, I shuddered in horror.

I couldn't move; couldn't scream. My eyes were drawn downward like lead to a magnet. Blinking, I edged a little closer to better examine the object. Air gusted from my lungs.

"It's a *rock,* you ninny," I chastised myself, jiggling it loose from its moorings. I hefted the grapefruit-sized lump, wishing it was small enough to keep as a souvenir of my overactive imagination.

As I brushed away the dirt, I noticed dark streaks mottling its creamy surface. My heart began pounding—harder than it had seconds before.

"Uh, Dick . . ."

"Darlin', are you hurt?" Ransom asked, rushing over. "That goddamned Joplin—"

"Dick, get over here!" The urgency in my voice matched the wind's lament. Ignoring Ransom completely, I scrambled to my feet.

"What the hell are you hollerin' about, missy? It's enough to wake—" Dick's teeth snapped together like a bear trap.

I cupped the stone in both hands and extended my arms toward him. Gracing me with an irritable scowl, he snatched it up and gave it a cursory glance. Then his head bowed and he examined it intently.

Garrett and Ransom crowded close, their chins hovered above Dick's shoulders. The Forty-Niner flung out his elbows.

"Christ, can you give a man room to breathe?" He spit on the stone, polished it with a sleeve, and squinted at it again.

"It's blossom rock, isn't it?" I whispered.

"Not exactly. It's quartz, though. Right heavy veining in it, too."

"For sure?" Ransom exclaimed. "Gold?"

Dick looked up, his expression solemn. "No doubt about it."

The wind sounded for all the world like sonorous, malevolent laughter. It seemed to mock us, daring us to intrude on its domain.

At any other time, in any other place, we'd have locked arms and danced a jubilant "Turkey in the Straw." But not here, in Butcher's Gulch, with the gruesome remains of its previous owners leering at us from unhallowed ground.

June. Tuesday, 4th, 1861

*Started out early, went almost to top of
mountain to get good dry wood. About half-
finished the cabin. Worked hard. I am
worse used up than I have been. Clear
and pleasant.*

I'd always scoffed at superstitions and haint stories, but that eerie, moaning wind did rob me of
a restful night's sleep. Judging by the smudgy
wattles beneath my partners' eyes, I wasn't the
only one who'd memorized every one of the Big
Dipper's sparkling facets.

Now, three hours past sunrise, we stood,
heads bowed, beside a lengthy mound of fresh-
turned dirt. There'd been not a word exchanged
regarding the Swedes' burial. Shovels and picks
were simply taken up after breakfast and the
gruesome deed was done.

"I'm no preacher, Lord," Garrett said, "but

I reckon these men are past needing one anyhow."

Clutching the locket and chain I'd found amid the jumbled remains, I blinked back tears. The tiny picture it held portrayed a light-eyed, moustachioed young man, a petite Dresden beauty at his side.

Garrett cleared his throat. "I don't know anything about these boys and don't need to. Whatever sins they may have committed, they didn't deserve to die the way they did. God bless them and keep them. Amen."

Dick secured a twine-lashed cross at one end of the mass grave. I knelt and draped the chain over its spire. The locket's plain, mellow face glowed like an amulet.

"Aren't you afraid it'll be stolen?" Ransom murmured as we turned to walk back to camp. "The rest of their plunder certainly was—no pun intended—spirited away."

Intended or not, I found his choice of words distasteful. I almost said as much, but instead answered curtly, "Maybe someone will happen along and recognize them from the picture. Identifying one would probably identify them all. That may be the only way their families will ever know what happened to them."

He dangled an unwanted arm across my shoulders. "You're a good woman, Abigail Fiske. Far too good for the likes of me."

"I'll not argue that."

Well, mercy me, I scolded silently, aren't we quite the shrew today?

Ransom glanced ahead at our partners' backs, then hustled me into a depression in the canyon wall.

"Oh, please, this isn't—" His lips interrupted in that deliciously seductive way he practiced to perfection. I wrapped my arms around his neck, arching my body against his.

Maybe I was fast, of questionable moral character, but I needed to feel womanly, desirable, and cared for beyond just another member of the partnership.

In all my twenty years, I'd never acknowledged my own mortality. It was sobering, frightening, to realize how fragile life was and how instantly and serendipitously it could end.

"Will you marry me, Abigail?" Ransom murmured. "Tell me now, is it yes or no?"

Visions of wondrous, passionate nights when time stood still and the real world didn't dare intrude made my heart yearn to say yes.

My head, an aggravating appendage at moments like this, hesitated at the ultimatum, warned that while we'd kept constant company for months, the circumstances were too extraordinary for an accurate sense of him. It also questioned whether I was truly ready for marriage, the inevitable children, and that much-despised phrase, "settling down."

"Why must you know this instant?"

His chin buckled stubbornly. "You either love me or you don't. If you do, there's no reason to wait."

I didn't respond. He must have taken that as an encouraging sign, for he brightened immediately. "I'm sure a minister of some denomination lives in Hattiesville. Or a circuit rider, perhaps. We'll say our vows Sunday afternoon, after regular services."

The weightless magic his kiss inspired evaporated like breath on a cold windowpane. "It's not that simple, Ransom. Love isn't enough to bind two people for a lifetime. Shared interests, goals—"

"Oh, for Christ's sake." He ran his fingers through his hair. "We've shared the same ambition since the day we met!"

"No, we haven't." I looked into his eyes as straight as a gambler bluffing a spade flush. "You're hell-bent to get rich. I only want to stop being poor."

Starting away, I paused when he lightly caught my wrist. "I don't understand the difference."

"I know you don't, Ransom. I don't think you ever will."

Easing from his grasp, I strolled toward camp alone, heart and head still waging an emotional donnybrook. What's wrong with me? Why am I so reluctant? Good heavens, most females my age would betroth themselves to any jake with two dollars for the license in his waistcoat.

Ransom likely thought as much, but I was not playing hard to get. I detested such frauds almost as much as their simpering perpetrators. Though I couldn't explain why, even to myself, his matrimonial badgering was vaguely disconcerting.

"Never buy anything from a man who's uncommonly eager to sell," Papa'd told me after he'd refused to part with a mere eight dollars for a gorgeous bay gelding I'd especially admired. Shortly thereafter, the horse dropped as dead as Paul Revere, which my stubborn pride dismissed as coincidence.

Oh, Papa, what I wouldn't give for your trusty ear and some of your horse sense right now.

I neared the smoldering campfire. Garrett had his back to me, stuffing my plump ore sample and smaller bits we'd found into a pack.

"About time you showed up," he snapped, glaring over his shoulder. "So where's your dearly beloved?"

His tone sparked my temper like a struck

match. "Ransom will be along directly, as if it's any of your business."

The pack thudded to the ground. Garrett wheeled, his expression livid. He leveled a finger at my chest.

"Everything that affects this company is my business, lady. You wanna hayroll that bootlicker, have the decency to do it after dark."

I slapped him so hard my palm stung on impact. "Don't you *ever*—"

Ransom ran up from behind and pushed me aside. He wadded Garrett's shirt in his fist. "What'd you call me, mister?"

Garrett cocked his head, bringing his left arm up for ballast. His right pulled back like an archer's.

Dick lunged between them, shoving them apart. "Give it a rest."

Sidling beyond his reach, Garrett warned, "Get out of the way, Curtis."

"What, you gonna fight me, too?" He jerked a thumb in my direction. "Maybe I oughta take a poke at her and get a real Jesse goin'."

Garrett's shoulders slumped. A sigh whistled low through his lips. Ransom looked away, his jaw muscles working furiously.

"That's more like it," Dick replied. Speaking to each in turn, he continued, "I know you fellers get lathered now and again. Mining camps bring out the best and the worst in folks. Gotta expect it. But real sudden-like, we're all strung tighter'n a washerwoman's clothesline."

"Can't argue that," Garrett admitted. His dark eyes pegged mine. "Abigail, I don't know what got into me, but I swear, I've never talked to a woman like that in my life. It damn sure won't happen again."

I waved a hand dismissively. "We let Opie put the spook to us, that's all. And if we're going to be tetchy whenever the wind blows and jump at every shadow, I think we'd best move on."

Dick shot me a withering look. "Aw, hell, gal, that fumadiddle's saddle won't dry out 'til Christmas. Just 'cause he believes them horse apples he shoveled at us don't mean we do."

The brawlers nodded solemnly, proving that Hattiesville's dithery mayor wasn't the only male of my acquaintance adept at manure-spreading.

Ransom offered his hand to Garrett. "What say we put our muscle to better use, like getting a roof over our heads."

Garrett clasped it. "Yeah. Maybe if we start living more civilized, we'll act that way."

Because none of us had been particularly eager to abandon the fire last night, we'd discussed building a small cabin before any mining was started.

"Sledging out tunnels is torture a-plenty without sleeping on a bed of rocks," Dick had cautioned. "Blankets don't knock much rain off'n a body, neither, and we're bound to get some frog-stranglers."

It was decided that Thursday would be soon enough to start harvesting Butcher's Gulch's lode of gilded quartz. Though it wasn't mentioned aloud, we younger, stouter partners would lumberjack while the senior member of our group had the samples assayed and recorded our claim.

With the urge for fisticuffs averted, Dick clopped toward town astride Stoophy while Ransom, Garrett, and I started climbing to the rim of the canyon.

Lugging axes, spare handles, and files, the men chattered with insufferable politeness, a common disguise for a sincere and mutual loathing.

Both totally ignored my presence, whereas hordes of stinging, biting, pestering insects lent their undivided attention. Occasionally, a downed branch set to wobbling by our passage sent my pulse racing. I wasn't terrified of snakes exactly, but preferred maintaining an extremely distant acquaintanceship with the slithering fiends.

Midway up the steep, cruel slope, I was compelled to ask Garrett why the cottonwood grove we'd passed yesterday on blessedly level ground wasn't a better choice for construction material.

"Because dragging half a forest a mile or three is a whole lot tougher than pitching it downhill to where you want it," he answered reasonably.

Once the felling commenced, despite the fact that past exertions had rendered me as robust as any man my size, every blow of that ten-ton ax jolted me from teeth to kneecaps. Before two trees surrendered to my awkward assaults, milled lumber's twelve-dollar-a-board-foot price seemed like the bargain of the century.

Dick rejoined us shortly after dinner, grinning as smugly as a cat with a mouse between its paws. "Lady and gents, this hunk of rock is o-fficially the prop-ity of Collingsworth and Company."

Holding an iron bar out to me, he waggled his fingers for my ax in trade. He then lofted the implement like a wine goblet, expelled a thunderous belch, and said, "May it ever provide and profit its, uh, illus-ter-ee-us owners."

Garrett peeled off his hat and sopped his sweaty brow with his sleeve. He sniffed the yeasty air. "You'd better have guzzled a coupla those beers for me, old-timer."

"Matter of factly, we raised steins to alla ya— me and Joplin, that is. Damned if I didn't misjudge ol' Opie. Thinks we're plumb loco for stayin' on, but the feller's right generous with a barrel o' Tivoli, by gum."

Ransom and Garrett exchanged wry glances, all but licking their lips with envy. I'd been told that frequently imbibing that bitter brew developed a taste for it. One sip of Papa's favorite brand had left me wondering why anyone would want to.

Dick squinted at the sun, tottering backward a few steps. "Best get on with this barn raisin' afore the moon comes up."

Shouldering my ax, he added, "Contrary to what you children think, I ain't got a foot in the grave yet. Whilst I'm a-proving it, the little woman there'll tidy the ridge by hefting them logs over the side with the jack—won'tcha, gal?"

Much as I wanted shed of that heavy, double-bladed demon, I asked, "Are you sure your elbow didn't get a bit too limber in town?"

The entire side of his face drew up comically when he winked. "Nah. I just warmed it up real good."

Praying that he'd sport the same number of toes tomorrow as he did today, I leveraged the iron bar beneath the tree nearest the rim.

Over the ringing thuds of axes biting into bark, Ransom shouted, "Hey, Dick—what'd you name this bonanza?"

The answer followed a lengthy pause. "Well,

accordin' to Opie, them foreigners called it Valhalla's Reward. That's Swede-lingo for soldiers' heaven or some such."

The ground shuddered with a solid stroke of the argonaut's ax. "Can't explain it, but licketysplit 'The Redemption' popped into my mind. Couldn't cogitate nothing better, so I stuck with it."

A trace of a smile curved my lips as the log rumbled down to the canyon floor. The Redemption. Yes, indeed, the name rolled very nicely off the tongue.

I chuckled to myself. Despite its history and even if the mine failed to live up to that lofty title, owning a quarter-share of The Redemption was certainly an improvement over owning a like fraction of a claim called The Gee Whiz.

June. Thursday, 13th, 1861

*Traveled down to the lake, stopped there
to get some fish. Overtook a strange
creature in the shape of a woman and took
a chat. Warm and pleasant.*

Decades of mining experience had given Dick a hard-knocks education in geology. Two weeks earlier, he'd put it to use when he scrutinized The Redemption's face.

"See the way them juxtaposits is heaved anti-goggling?" he asked we three apprentices, pointing at the canyon wall's misaligned bands of white, rose, tan, and gray.

I hadn't noticed before, but the seams didn't run parallel for more than a few yards. It was as if Mother Nature had sliced the bluff into sections and stitched them together again with her eyes closed.

"The vein, if there is one, will zigzag same as

the rock it's hiding in," he explained. "I reckon we're more likely to hit it if each of us digs a coyote shaft about fifty feet apart instead of us picking out the same one."

I remembered Ransom stroking his jaw, one eyebrow pursed like a cold caterpillar. "Sounds like a lot more work to me."

"Uh-huh," Garrett had snorted. "That's the same thing you said when I told you to notch those logs careful so the cabin walls'd fit tight."

"And I did as I was told, didn't I, Father Collingsworth? In fact, our shack was as quiet as a—" Ransom sputtered a mite, then sneered, "Well, we didn't hear that godawful wind caterwauling all night, anyway."

To date, we'd spent fourteen days chipping tunnels in the canyon's flinty surface. During that time, if my ears weren't ringing from the ping of steel pounding rock, they flinched from Ransom and Garrett's continual quarreling or the racket of three men snoring to beat Billy thunder in an eight-by-ten cabin.

One might assume that eventually Garrett and Ransom would become too exhausted to taunt each other. To the contrary, that the mining technique we'd engaged in was called "coyoting" seemed doubly appropriate since they constantly nipped at each other like prairie wolves chasing the same jackrabbit.

I got a bellyful at dinner today and it wasn't the kind that comes from an overindulgence in flapjacks, bacon, and tinned tomatoes, either.

Fork tines rasped against tin as Ransom scooped up the pooled dregs of molasses. "What's the deal, Garrett? Are we running low on batter makings?"

"Nope."

"Is there any left?"

"I don't rightly remember."

Ransom kicked back the bench and stomped outside to cookfire. His shadow hadn't disappeared before his body filled the threshold again.

"There's not a scrap of anything out here. You can't expect me to do a full day's work on half a plate of food."

Dick's eyes never wavered from the sickly pink tomato on his plate. No more attention than he paid to the ongoing battles; he could've lived in a root cellar with fourteen children and sworn his wife was barren.

"Here, Ransom, take some of mine," I offered.

"Yeah, Halsey. Stoke up on her dinner if it'll get a full day's work out of you for once."

Ransom stopped in midstride. "What's that supposed to mean?"

"It means we all started our drifts at the same time, except yours wouldn't keep the rain off a runt cub. Hell, Abigail's number three shaft is twice the size of your number four."

Ignoring the backhanded compliment, I gripped the table's split-log edge. "Would you two please quit bickering so we can have a meal in peace for once?"

Ransom bellowed, "God*damn,* I'm sick of you calling me a shiftless—"

"More like 'shaftless,' from where I sit."

My palms slapped the rough pine. "I've had all I can stand of both of you." Snatching Dick's willow fishing pole from its pegs, I started for the door.

"Ransom, there'll be fish a-plenty for supper tonight to shut you up about the victuals. Garrett, my father said the only thing you get out of a whipped slave is a funeral. If you don't like the way things are done around here, you can damn well do them yourself."

Sucking in a lungful of air, I added, "As for you, Mr. Curtis . . . well, you're nothing but a deaf, dumb old coot and right now, I don't like you very much, either."

I caught a glimpse of three stupefied faces before I flounced out. Hell hath no fury like a riled, redheaded woman, I paraphrased, my temper cooling as quickly as it'd flared.

Dick had told us about a small stream-fed lake he'd literally stumbled into on the way back from

Hattiesville the day he registered our claim. Promising a trout fry, he'd cut and rigged the willow pole, but swinging a pick from daylight to dusk had left no leisurely hours for fishing.

Beyond the confines of Butcher's Gulch, the lush, verdant slope was strewn with wildflowers and iris spears; their blossoms still rolled tight like pointed pastel cigars. To the east, the mountains taunted the clouds' fluffy hulls, snow-capped peaks and cottony vapor all but indistinguishable.

The sun caressed my face. Turmoil and years fell away and I was a young, carefree girl again, exploring the world's wonders. I marveled at birds twittering in the trees and gliding effortlessly across the sky, at the heady aroma of dew-kissed loam, at myriad colors and contours vying for my attention.

I laughed at the antics of a yellow-bellied marmot family. Rearing on their haunches like gold-flecked miniature bears, they wrestled and butted each other with their blunt, bewhiskered snouts. Their loud, boisterous chirps explained their "whistle pig" nickname.

Stuffing my grubby cap in my pocket, I shook out my hair so it could frolic in the breeze. Strands teased my lips and tickled across my cheeks like spider webs.

The lake, actually no more than a narrow

aquamarine pool, nestled in a quaking aspen grove where the stream paused to collect itself before rushing through the foothills.

On the bank, a supple buckskin trailing its reins was lazily nuzzling clumps of lacy ferns and marsh marigolds. Had I believed such creatures existed, I'd have thought the hourglass-shaped figure spit-bathing nearby was a barefooted wood nymph.

Lifting her head to wring a sodden handkerchief at her neck, cornsilk hair so pale it appeared to be white fanned to her waist, almost hiding her chemise. Standing several inches shy of five feet tall, if not for those womanly curves, she'd have easily been mistaken for a child.

To prevent frightening her, I scuffled my boots as I approached. The black-and-tan horse craned its neck toward me and whickered. Its owner spun around and shielded her bosom behind crossed forearms.

"Good afternoon, ma'am. I'm sorry if I startled you."

The smile spreading across her heart-shaped face would've made an angel envious. Brilliant jade sloe-eyes beckoned me closer. "I'll admit, the last thing I expected to see was another woman."

She surveyed my mannish attire and laughed. "A few minutes ago, I was dressed just like you.

Skirts and saddles don't mix but for Sunday afternoon jaunts."

"You've traveled a distance, then?"

"Oh, yes." One slender arm disappeared into the sleeve of a pink, tuck-pleated blouse, which lessened the severity of her voluminous charcoal skirt. "Aboard the stage from Kearny, Nebraska and astride from Denver City."

She glanced at my fishing gear. "I presume you live close by, Missus . . . ?"

I corrected the marital status with my introduction. "My parents and I are working a claim about three miles up the draw."

"Really? My husband's prospecting in this vicinity, too! Maybe you've run across him—" Her lips puckered into a charming pout. "Mercy, I've forgotten my manners entirely."

Extending a dainty hand, she said, "I'm Missus Ransom Halsey, but please, call me Bettina."

I clasped her hand limply, staring as if she'd just sprouted fangs and horns. Ransom's . . . wife? My knees threatened to buckle. Yes, that "missus," had been spoken quite clearly and she damn sure wasn't his mother. Bile scalded my throat. I was too angry to cry, too hurt to think straight.

Bettina eased her fingers from my grasp. "What's wrong?" she asked, regarding me quizzically. The blood drained from her face. "You *do* know Ransom. Something's happened to him, hasn't it? Abigail, please—answer me."

Her terrified voice broke through my mental haze. "I assure you, Ransom and Garrett Collingsworth were scrapping like alley cats when I left our camp a while ago."

"Thank God." Her eyes closed and she sighed with relief. "So you're a member of Collingsworth and Company? Of course—Fiske, wasn't it? Ransom mentioned a man by that name in his letters."

Letters. He'd written her letters while he courted me. I clenched my fists behind my back, willing myself to stay calm.

"My father died before we reached Denver City, Bettina. I suppose you could say I'm his proxy."

She expressed condolences as she bent to hastily tug on glossy, patent-leather oxfords exactly like those I dreamed I'd buy for myself someday.

"Will you take me to my husband, Abigail? We haven't seen each other in months and I'd so enjoy talking with you on the way."

If only she were ugly, grossly fat, or a sharp-tongued harpy, I could dislike her. Ransom would still be a loathsome, lying cad, but that might excuse his behavior a tiny degree.

I wanted to expose her husband's duplicity—

not to inflict the same pain on her that was coursing through me, but because she deserved a far better man than Ransom Halsey.

Before I realized what I was saying, the devil in me agreed to lead Bettina to The Redemption. There was no logical reason to refuse, and frankly, I couldn't resist being a witness to their undoubtedly surprise reunion.

She dashed off to stow her riding boots and trail-grimy clothing in the saddlebags. Scooping up the buckskin's reins, she geed him into a jogging gait and rejoined me.

"Those boardwalk shoes'll cripple you before we get to camp," I warned. "Besides, it's silly to walk when you can ride."

"Honestly, my sitter-downer has almost worn through to my lap. I'll welcome a good stretch of the legs."

We strolled several yards in silence, suddenly and inexplicably shy. A thousand meddlesome questions hatched in my brain, but I'd never had a talent for chitchat even under the most innocuous circumstances.

"It must be hard for you," Bettina said softly. "I mean, being left to fend for yourself among three men you'd never met. At times, being forever outnumbered by a father-in-law, a husband, and two sons is enough to make me want to lock myself in the privy for an afternoon."

Two sons, eh? Ransom once told me he wanted a dozen children. He never mentioned how many wives he planned to take to produce them. I forced my mind off that track before I lost the conversational thread entirely.

"That's why I'm here and not pounding sandstone with a pickax as I should be," I said. "It was either take wing or take a club to all three of my irascible partners."

Concern clouded Bettina's expression. "I've heard dark rumors about that claim. If not for Butcher's Gulch's jinxed reputation, I'd have never found you."

"Ghost stories or no, it's a miracle you did. I couldn't locate where we are on a map, let alone where we've been or how we got here."

The proud tilt of her chin matched her jaunty stride as she recounted being introduced to Father Dyer. He'd remembered our brief encounter and heard through the miner's grapevine that "a crazy jasper, name of Collingsworth" had staked out the infamous Butcher's Gulch.

Countless rehashings of the Swedes' mysterious, gory demise in saloons and around campfires had not only blown the story completely out of proportion, it was now as much a part of Colorado history as Zebulon Pike's discovery of the peak named in his honor.

"I soon learned not to ask for directions to the

gulch proper because those I inquired of considered it the same as sending a bullet through my fair heart," Bettina said with a chuckle. "When one gent let it slip that Hattiesville was the closest town, I simply altered my stated destination."

Astonished that an extraordinary measure of shrewdness and grit came wrapped in such a petite, delicate package, I gawked at her in unabashed admiration.

"Lawsy, Bettina. You've got more sand than the Sahara. This territory's treacherous enough for a man to roam, much less a woman."

"Truthfully, Abigail, much as I appreciate the flattery, it wasn't gumption that brought me five hundred miles from home."

When she continued, her tone held a bitter edge. "If Ransom had met me in Denver City on May tenth—our anniversary—as he'd promised, I'd be in Kearny with my little boys and coaxing Jed—that's Ransom's father—to stay abed and take his medicine."

Odd that a wealthy Pennsylvania steel magnate would be convalescing in Nebraska, I thought. "The elder Mr. Halsey isn't seriously ill, I hope."

Bettina's gossamer mane danced on the breeze when she waggled her head. "It's the pneumonia, worsened by exhaustion. Jed's been dispirited ever since Ransom's mother died crossing the plains when we moved from Missouri five years ago.

"I'd hoped the success of Halsey and Son's Fast Freight might keep him too busy to grieve, but it didn't. After Ransom left for Colorado, the poor man worked twenty hours a day trying to manage the business alone.

"Jed doesn't trust hired help, won't sell what he considers his son's legacy, and won't bolt the doors until his health recovers. I had no choice but to find Ransom and take him back before his father keels over dead."

Mentally, I added a few more derogatory adjectives befitting Ransom's complete lack of character. A two-legged chameleon. The greatest actor to never tread a stage. A flesh and bone statue lacking any trace of compassion, morality, or sense of right and wrong.

How he'd beguiled Bettina I'd never know, but how he so easily and effectively conned a con man's daughter made my blood boil at my own stupidity. I trembled with rage and couldn't stop.

I remembered Papa rationalizing his fraudulent pursuits by saying, "I don't lie to people as much as I tell them what they most want to hear, Abigail.

"The suffering want relief from pain, regardless of whether it comes from a deity or a doctor.

Believing such things are possible is more soothing than harmful.

"During a drought, farmers would sell their souls to the devil for an inch of rain. My machine gives two weeks' worth of hope to the hopeless. If the skies remain clear, at least they feel they'd done something to alleviate the situation rather than knuckle under to despair."

If "sincere charlatan" was not a total conflict in terms, Papa had surely been one. He'd never intentionally hurt anyone.

Maybe Ransom's affection for me was based on a similar, absolving pretense. Like Papa's customers, I believed his declarations because I wanted desperately for them to be true.

A deeper sense of how M. R. T. Fiske's sheep felt upon comprehending the shearing they'd been given added tonnage to an already heavy heart.

"Let's take a rest, Bettina," I suggested, pointing to a spreading Gambel oak. "We've got a steeper climb ahead of us and you are beginning to limp."

She grimaced at her dusty boots. "Can't say you didn't warn me, can I?"

I tethered the buckskin to a low-hanging branch to graze. Bettina untied a blanket lashed to the saddle's cantle and laid it in the shade.

She spent an uncommonly long time arranging

and fussing with her petticoats and skirt. Suddenly, those slanted cat's eyes looked boldly into mine. "It's funny, isn't it, how we confide things to strangers that we wouldn't divulge to close friends."

"Maybe it's because secrets told to folks we'll never see again can't come back to haunt us. It's a second cousin to talking things over with yourself."

That Cupid's smile brightened her face again. "Except nobody'll think you're addlepated if they hear you."

"Nothing you've told me will be repeated, Bettina." I squeezed her forearm gently. "That's a promise."

"I knew you wouldn't. But will you tell me something, in confidence?"

My breath caught in my throat. I was sure she was about to ask whether Ransom and I were romantically involved. Should I lie to prevent hurting her? Or answer truthfully out of respect?

Her inquiry took me completely aback. "What has Ransom told you about me?"

The intuition that had failed miserably at exposing Ransom for the prevaricator he was, screamed for reparations. A strong hunch that he lacked the imagination to pull a bogus life history from thin air urged me to take a gamble.

"If I recall correctly, he said you come from

Philadelphia and that your father is involved in the steel industry."

"That figures. Much as I love my husband, I'm not blind to his incurable need to preen. I'll bet he failed to mention that Father disinherited me after we married."

"That's ter—"

She held up her hand to hush me. "My father isn't entirely unreasonable. His ultimatum, which I didn't believe and promptly ignored, put him in a corner. Stubborn pride kept him there."

I snorted indelicately. "You're a better woman than I, Bettina. I'd have told dear old Dad where to put his filthy old smelter—among other things."

"The passage of five years hasn't changed his opinion of Ransom, but Father knows he has two grandsons growing as fast as winter wheat. I have a feeling there'll be a letter soon, saying he's coming West on business as if the breach never occurred."

"I hope you're right." My knees crackled when I stood and stretched. "Speaking of ultimatums, you're going to sidesaddle that gelding the rest of the way to Butcher's Gulch, and I don't mean maybe."

Bettina draped the blanket over one arm and saluted with the other. "Yes, ma'am, and bless your kind heart."

A half hour later, the clang of shod hooves on the rocky canyon's floor brought my partners out of their respective burrows like prairie dogs.

Garrett and Dick looked mildly curious.

Ransom dropped his pick and tottered backward against his tunnel's entrance. I hadn't seen a man who appeared more ready for an undertaker's services since Mordechai McMillen gut-shot Comanche Joe Demerest in Boone City, Kansas.

Until that moment, I'd never tasted revenge. God forgive me, but it was *powerfully* sweet.

June. Saturday, 15th, 1861

*Dick going to a ball tonight. Borrowed a
shirt, boots, coat and vest, all to go to a
$2 ball. My hands very sore. Pleasant.*

A lad of about sixteen galloped into camp this
morning. Breathless, and with eyes gleaming
more white than hazel, he delivered Opie Joplin's
gratis invitation to tonight's miner's ball. It was
no sooner given than the boy wheeled his piebald
and skedaddled.

I pondered whether some toe-tapping fiddle
music and a few quadrilles across a sawdusty
dance floor might cure my dauncy mood. Two
days' worth of pretending the crags in my tunnel's walls represented various parts of Ransom
Halsey's anatomy and demolishing them forth-
with hadn't done anything besides raise watery
blisters on my palms.

Garrett concealed his anticipation of a social

event by shrugging his shoulders, but Dick obviously considered it a special occasion. He skipped supper altogether, heading for the washtub in the brush arbor to "teach my nits and ticks how to swim."

Judging by the bawdy Irish ditty bellowing from that direction, he wasn't suffering overmuch from an application of soap and water.

The argonaut's enthusiasm abetted my decision not to inflict my grouchy self on innocent townsfolk. Parties were, after all, where people go to express happiness, not mercantiles where the morose can acquire a fresh supply.

Wearing relatively clean woolen drawers, Dick emerged from the harbor as pink and sweet-smelling as a babe. In quick order, he climbed into his least filthy overalls, a red flannel shirt Garrett donated to the cause, plus his best boots—with socks stuffed in their toes to give Dick some hope of keeping the clodhoppers on his feet. To complete the beggar's godawful ensemble, I contributed Papa's prized green-and-ocher tapestry vest.

Astride Stoophy's blanketed back, hair slicked by a dab of bacon grease, and swaddled in his borrowed, comically oversized clothing, Dick looked like a creek turtle rigged up in a terrapin's shell.

"Ain't I just too purty to live? No wonder ya'll

ain't going with me. Can't stand the competition."

"Watch your tail—and your front, for that matter—when you stagger home from town," Garrett cautioned. "We don't know what flavor of redskins have been watching us lately."

Dick nodded and heeled the mule's barreled flanks. "There is a house in New Orleans," he wailed tunelessly, "They call it the Rising Sun . . ."

Garrett and I exchanged bemused grins as the stanzas faded into the dusk. "Has been the ruin of many a boy . . . good God, an' I am one . . ."

Mumbling something about accounts to reconcile, Garrett strode to the cabin. Our windowless, slightly whomperjawed shack's design defied howling winds and winged, bloodsucking critters. Except not a breath of air stirred between those mud-chinked log walls and unless I was ripe for the pillow, the shelter was more cage than comfort.

I ambled north, preferring the Gulch's moaning ghosts to feeling like a firefly trapped in a jar. The three-quarter moon glistened like a silver filigree brooch on cobalt velvet. Hoot owls, coyote choirs, rustles, and chirrups echoed from the shadows.

Splaying my elbows atop Stoophy's split-rail corral, I peered down the canyons murky throat.

Thursday instant, after the Halsey's departed for Hattiesville and the room Bettina'd let for the night at the hotel, I'd told my remaining partners to leave me to brood by myself.

Oddly enough, other than "G'morning," "G'night," or "How about passing that tallow butter?" Garrett and Dick had all but ignored me ever since.

"Damned if I'll ever understand men," I muttered at the moon. "Guess there's no use expecting sympathy from any sons of Adam."

As had become its custom, left to its own devices, my heart began shuffling emotions and memories like a deck of *E. Pluribus Unums*. Flashes of Ransom's ardor, his devious machinations, his caresses, and his words of love taunted me.

"Lies—all of it lies." I rocked my chin on my knuckles, trying to defeat yet another stream of tears.

Ransom admitted as much when he'd insisted upon speaking to me privately. "I don't expect you to believe me, but I swear on my mother's grave, I wasn't lying when I told you I loved you and that I wanted to spend the rest of my life with you."

A bitter gust had chuffed between my lips. "And I suppose my infinite charms flat wiped the memory of a wife and two children clean from your mind, eh?"

The bastard had the unmitigated gall to sound anguished when he replied, "Dick told me The Redemption was as sure to yield a strike as he'd ever seen. I'd hoped we'd make a new life, a fresh start, together."

"God-Almighty-damn, what a stupid, insufferable fool you are. You already have the most precious sure thing any man could want: a woman and two sons that love you in spite of yourself."

"Abigail—"

"Bettina's waiting for you. Good-bye, Ransom, and may you rot in hell."

Suddenly it struck me as no coincidence that I'd turned my back to the direction he and Bettina had taken from Butcher's Gulch. Squaring my shoulders, I crossed my arms over my chest and told the stars above that I'd cried all I was going to for handsome Ransom Halsey.

"By God, I haven't lost a thing besides a little self-respect, and there's plenty left to sustain me. That Judas goat I featured myself in love with will never have a jot of it to call his own."

Footsteps crunched behind me. Lawsy, how that noise raised every hair on the back of my neck. Before the whim-whams completely paralyzed me, I chanced a peek out of the corner of my eye.

In the moonlight, Garrett's burly silhouette really did resemble a grizzly's. The fact that bears roaming in this neck of the woods rarely wore slouch hats was all that saved me from a premature demise.

"Air's a bit nippy," he said. "I brought you a coat." He held it by the lapels so I could slip my arms into the sleeves. As I shrugged my shoulders to situate the garment, his hands gently freed my hair of the collar.

A knot formed in my throat. Papa used to do that when I was a little girl. I hadn't realized how much I'd missed that tender, courtly gesture.

"Thank you . . . Garrett."

He scuffled the dust in a decidedly "Aw, shucks" manner, mumbled "Don't mention it," and turned to leave.

"I'd welcome some company."

Reversing himself, he studied me for a long moment. "You sure?"

"Absolutely. I'm so tired of my own, I was about to start singing along with the coyotes."

Garrett stuck his hands in his pockets and rocked back on his heels. "Nice evening, isn't it? Wonder if ol' Dick's having a high time cutting his wolf loose."

I chuckled at the image of that skinny scarecrow do-si-doing with a buxom calico queen.

"Something tells me he's having a ball. So to speak."

"Just so he doesn't get corn-stupid."

I scanned the bosky ridges. Feeble moonlight blurred their familiar contours. Thoughts that an army could lurk there without being seen sent gooseflesh rollicking up my arms.

"Do you really think we're in danger?"

He sniffed dismissively. "Nah. Just curious about what those redskins are so curious about, that's all."

An uneasy silence got us both fidgeting. As people are wont to do in these situations, we blurted a word or two at the same time, paused, extended "What were you saying?" "No, you go ahead" courtesies, and fell mute again.

"Guess we'd best clear our craws of what's stuck in them before we choke," Garrett said.

I started to respond, but his expression told me he hadn't finished clearing his.

"Abigail, I'm sorry for the hurt Ransom caused you. Mostly, I'm sorry for letting you to chew your cud all by your lonesome."

"There's nothing to apologize for—"

"Oh, yes, there is. I never liked the son of a bitch and made no secret of it. But after we got caught in that blizzard, I was as spiteful to you as I was to him. That ain't the way a friend treats a friend."

"As if I've acted any better? Sure, Ransom did his best to make me distrust you. The most shameful thing I've ever done was listen to him. I didn't believe all he said, but I did listen, Garrett."

His brown eyes softened. I could see I wasn't the only one hurt by Ransom's lies. "Trust isn't won, gal, it's earned. Lillith told me to never trust anyone that tried to tell me how to think. I reckon Ransom taught you the same lesson, the hard way."

"Maybe so, but damned if I'll thank him for it. Can we make a deal, Mr. Collingsworth?"

"What kind of a deal?" he asked suspiciously.

"To do our best to forget that double-dealing jackass was ever a member of this company."

He swatted at a mosquito, a lazy grin playing across his lips. "Well, seeing as how he signed over all rights to The Redemption, I reckon we can."

It would take a while for Ransom to fade from memory, whether his nickname ranked mention or not. Asking that it not be was childish and vengeful. I was delighted that Garrett was amendable to the idea.

"No offense intended," I teased, "but if I'd known you better, Ra—*he* couldn't have bamboozled me so easily."

"Uh-uh, little lady. Think I don't know there's

a pinch of bamboozle in you, too? Try again. This time, off the top of the deck."

My bewildered, innocent moue had no more affect than the flinty glare I tried next. The brute seemed positively invincible to my best, womanly wiles.

"All right. I want to know more about you. And Lillith."

He nodded. "Fair enough, but let's go inside before the bugs drain us dry."

Within minutes, we were seated at the table with cups of syrupy black coffee cooling between our elbows.

Garrett pondered the whiskers of dry grass poking through the cracks in the split-timbered ceiling. When he spoke, it was as much to himself as to me.

"Pa and Mama drowned when I was four. A flash flood washed out the bridge and their wagon along with it. We'd never had much more'n a pot to piss in and a window to throw it through, but Lillith swore and be damned she wouldn't let anybody take me away and lock me in an orphanage."

He paused and took a sip of coffee. His face reflected both his admiration for Lillith and the price paid for resurrecting demons. "She was only fifteen. Couldn't find a job that paid squat. A whore name of Gertie took one look at Lillith and said she'd make a fortune in Kansas City. Gertie had a friend there that'd take Lillith in and teach her the tricks of the trade."

"The poor girl was hardly more than a child."

Garrett sighed deeply, his eyes boring into mine. "I don't reckon Lillith ever got to be a child. Seems Pa saw to that."

A fingertip traced circles in the wood. "Anyhow, Lillith did her best to take care of me and take care of business, without letting on exactly what her business was. Whenever she left the boardinghouse, her hair was all primped and curled and she smelled of lemon verbena. Told me she was a 'demimondaine.' Sounded right elegant to me. Didn't know for a long time that it was a fancy word for Jezebel."

"How'd you find out?"

He leaned back and laughed. "The same way boys learn what wonders gals hide under their petticoats, relations between men and women, all that stuff. Shoot, there's a heap more educating that goes on behind a schoolhouse than inside one."

"I'll bet some noses got bloodied when they told you what your sister did for a living."

"Yeah," he shot back, wincing. "Mine, mostly. And damned if Lillith didn't wale me later for fighting, too. So much for defending her honor."

The poignancy of that statement tugged at my

heart. Regardless of the adage, bruises left by sticks and stones did heal eventually, but playmates' cruel taunts are remembered for a lifetime.

"Above all else, my sister is an eternal, infernal pragmatist and doesn't need me or anybody else to defend her. Over the years, I've hated Lillith for being a whore, loved her for being herself, and tried like hell to make a martyr out of her. It's taken a while, but I finally quit judging her for what she does and just love her dearly for who she is."

I clasped my hands in my lap, wanting for all the world to jump up and hug the stuffing out of him. Not knowing how he'd react, I stifled the impulse by asking, "Did you know that Lillith and my father knew each other?"

"Oh, they more than knew each other. It appears I was two shakes from being, what? Let's see, if my sister'd married your father, that'd have made me your . . . uncle?"

"Papa's brother-in-law is as far as I got. Uncle Garrett, huh? I think I'd have liked that."

He curried his mustache and regarded me thoughtfully. Actually, his expression was a nonce wicked. I didn't need a gypsy to divine what he was thinking.

"Well, then, if Papa and Lillith were so fond of each other, why didn't they marry?"

Bench legs scraped across the dirt floor. Garrett rose to his feet like a stoved-up codger. "I'll give you the same answer Lillith gave me: It's none of your concern."

He groaned as he stretched so fully his palms grazed the rafters. I plopped my chin in my hand. "Shall I assume this delightful repartee is over?"

"Sorry, little gal, but there'll be others, I promise. The past coupla days have been pretty wearisome for this old pick-swinger, too."

"Would you mind if I asked you one more thing?"

"Hmmph. Anything short of sudden death gonna stop you?"

I waggled my head.

"Have at it, then."

"Why'd you put this company together? More importantly, why are you so dogged-determined to strike it rich?"

His knees popped as he settled onto the end of the bench. "That's two questions, but since I'm such a helluva fine fella, I'll answer 'em both. Now, this isn't a judgment, it's fact. I want the Collingsworth name attached to something besides a dead lecher I don't even remember and the deed to El Dorado Parlor-Saloon.

"Someday, I want a wife and children, but not until I'm sure they'd never have to beg at back doors for table leavings if something happened to me.

"Lastly, though Lillith is a wealthy woman in her own right, she's terrified of winding up beggar-poor again. A piece of a gold mine can't repay what she'd given me, but it'll do for a start."

Scratching a welt on his neck, he yawned like a sun-warm mountain lion. "Can I find the blankets now, ma'am?"

I smiled through the guilt I felt for ever having doubted him, mixed with gratitude for being allowed me a peek at both his past and his future. "Good night, and sleep well."

"Best be finding your bunk, too, partner."

"I will."

He shuffled toward the corner of the room, hands massaging the bowed small of his back.

"Uh, Garrett?"

A low groan preceded a dismayed "What?"

"Thank you for a lovely evening."

He turned, grinned wanly, and said, "Abigail, the pleasure was truly all mine."

June. Sunday, 16th, 1861

*Hailed like sixty this morning about 10
o'clock, got home about 2 o'clock and
found the Gulch dry as a bone. Got
supper. Cloudy.*

My neck muscles were taut as a fat lady's corset
laces after only two hours' work in number three
shaft. With a hammer gripped in one fist and a
chisel in the other, I'd hardly commence a pert
rhythm before stopping, backing up, and craning
my head outside to peer down the canyon.

Now and again, my hearing played mean tricks
on me. I'd imagine I heard Stoophy's drizzly
snorts. Hooves *ka-thack*ing on stone. That ban-
shee whine Dick called singing. But checks and
rechecks didn't find even a black squirrel stirring
about in Butcher's Gulch.

Earlier, when he'd noticed Dick's bunk was
empty, Garrett's expression took on that graven

statue effect I'd seen on occasion. We hardly spoke during breakfast, both of us repeatedly cocking an ear toward the door.

"For heaven's sake. Dick got by many a year without either of us fretting over him," I said, trying to reassure myself as much as my frowning partner.

"Yeah, and you'd be more convincing without that green-apple bellyache look to you." Coffee slopped on the table when he banged his cup down. "He'll come crawling into camp directly. Let's get to work."

As morning wore on, I caught many a glimpse of Garrett's faded flannel shirt disappearing into number two's jagged arch. Had anyone seen us popping in and out of our respective tunnels, they'd probably have likened us to those horrid cuckoo clocks the German immigrants held so dear.

"Get your rifle, little gal."

My chisel clanked to the floor, missing my toes by a whisker. Garrett stood spraddle-legged a few feet from me, hands anchored to hips, glowering. "We're going hunting for a slat-sided Forty-Niner."

"I thought you said yesterday that one of us had best stay in camp at all times in case those Indians are hankering for our provisions."

He grunted. "That was yesterday. I'll not leave

you alone, nor send you to town that way, either."

Without snow to hobble him, that long-legged gent ambulated downhill as fast as a hungry dog after a gut-wagon. Truth to tell, he was so worried about Dick's whereabouts, I think he forgot all about the winded woman straggling behind him.

Murky clouds hovering overhead threatened a second bath in as many days. Altitude and the great drafts of sultry air I sucked in smoldered in my lungs. My ribs felt like barrel staves bound by chime hoops.

We were catcornering through a meadow when the thunderheads ruptured timidly. Here and there, hailstones the size of stone cherries hopped merrily, then scurried under lupine-leaf umbrellas.

Seconds later, a roaring barrage catapulted from the above. Garrett disappeared in the deluge. I dropped to my knees and curled into a tight ball. Frozen marbles pelted me from skull to hindquarters. If only my hands were as large as Garrett's, I could have bowled them like a helmet to protect my battered head.

Nigh as quickly as it began, the hailstorm abated as if a heavenly hatch had been pulled closed. Feeble shafts of sunlight caressed the cobbled white ground. The deliciously cool, gentle breeze was like an elder sister sent to apologize for her little brother's mischief-making.

"Whew. That was a right good noggin-thumping," Garrett said, staggering toward me.

The world wobbled a mite when I gained my feet, too. It was hard to feature such smallish pellets could pack such a painful wallop.

"You all right to travel?"

I nodded, taking a gingered step on the slick, rolly surface. "Dick's probably suffering a hellacious hangover, but wait'll I get ahold of him. I'll tan his hide and sell it for shoe leather for causing us so much misery."

"No sign of him yet, that's a fact. I'm suspecting he found a skir—uh, a table to crawl under for the night."

We doddered as awkwardly as ducks on dry land the remaining distance to Hattiesville. Once, Garrett's boots swooped from under him and he crashed square on his tailbone.

I doubled over, laughing so hard that tears spilled down my cheeks. He, however, didn't seem to find much humor in it.

We passed a smattering of shanties clinging tenuously to the foothills before we arrived in Hattiesville proper. Slopes where trees had survived and thrived for centuries were now bleak, eroding hogbacks bristling with raw stumps.

Farther on, if not for a half dozen false-fronted

clapboard buildings hugging the town's only street, I'd have thought a wagon train had careened down the mountain, strewing timber, house goods, and canvas bedcovers with every turn.

Boiled drawers and blankets danced from clotheslines strung between tents and cabins more crude than our own. Somewhere, a Jews' harp gave a free concert, though its player had only mastered one song.

I wrinkled my nose at the stench of human waste, animal dung, rotting garbage, and smoldering cookfires. Denver City smelled like a rose garden in comparison.

At the center of town, lashed to a towering fir trunk stripped of its branches, the Stars and Bars hung limply above the Stars and Stripes.

The visible proof of a nation divided saddened me beyond words. Women weren't supposed to understand such things and perhaps I did not, but this war, like all others fought throughout history, seemed a terribly high price to pay just to prove an opinion.

I turned my attention to a fancy, scroll-lettered sign trumpeting THE FOUNDERS BLOCK. Beneath it, a spacious roofed pavilion was wedged between a saloon and combination mercantile, recorder's, and mayor's office.

"Opie gave this wide spot a name and platted

her real fine," Garrett observed, "only I don't figure Hattiesville to ever amount to more'n a place to sleep, buy provisions, and fritter away a Saturday night."

I pointed at the American House Saloon. "I'll bet a month's pay we'll find that old coot in there."

"Think so?" He stroked his chin. "Well, if he's not and we hit color before mid-July, I'll hold you to that, little gal."

Groups of two to six circled the saloon's tables, loudly discussing what was wrong with the country and how easily it could be put to rights. Voices droning like hived bees rose to meet the cigar smoke that valanced the rafters.

The amateur Patrick Henrys paid no mind to Garrett and me as we sauntered to the untended bar at the room's far end. Keeping our backs turned and our mouths shut assured they would not.

"I hear Confederate agents is givin' forty dollars apiece for Navy Colts."

"Hmmph. Dragoons and rifles is bringin' a passel more'n that."

"Sure 'nough?" a graveled drawl inquired. "You know, sudden-like, there's been a powerful lot of gold shipments and strongboxes gettin' robbed onna way to Denver City, too. Kindee odd, ain't it?"

I caught Garrett's eye in the back-bar mirror. He shrugged and shook his head slightly, warning me not to ask any questions of the customers, or of him.

"It's the Union blockades what's causin' it." The elderly speaker's accent was as thick as cotton bolls. "Bad enough the South can't bring goods in. Worse, not shipping any of hers out."

"Aw, don't get your dander up, Willy Dean," called a younger jasper from an adjacent table. "President Davis's sleeves ain't empty and neither's his head. "If'n it's a fatter war chest he's needin', he knows where the gold is."

"Mark my words," opined another. "Davis'll give General Sibley marching orders any day now and Texas ain't more'n a good leg stretch from here."

Confederate soldiers invade Colorado? We'd heard so little about the war that it seemed a world away and, frankly, none of our concern. Yet, if these men were right, the territory would be drawn into the fracas.

Before I could ponder that frightening prospect, Opie Joplin waddled from the storeroom lugging a carton of gilt-labeled bottles. Dressed in a garish, bunting-striped vest with his moonlike face beaming above a fresh collar, he resembled a barber pole with arms.

"Well, if this isn't a welcome surprise," he

greeted, waggling a plump finger at me. "Your absence last night shattered many a lonely miner's heart, Miss Fiske."

"Better that than their toes," I replied, knowing full well that war talk had probably all but drowned out the music. "It's Dick Curtis's absence that's brought us into town, Opie."

The enterprising, part-time barkeep sopped his brow with a corner of his apron. "Him and four or five others took out last night for the Last Chance. That's a placer camp about fifteen miles east of here."

"Trouble?" Garrett shot back curtly.

Opie almost whispered his response. "Truth or rumor, it ain't good for bizness, nohow. This feller lurched in durin' the dance, a-hollerin' that Cheyenne had raided their camp. He'd lit out when the whoopin' commenced and run hell-bent-for-election to town. Dick and them other boys went back there with him to bury the dead and patch up the livin'."

Thoughts of our feathered watchers sent a chill clear through me. "Why would Indians raid a mining camp? They've no use for the gold."

"Tribes squabblin' amongst themselves mighta got their blood up," he answered grimly. "The Utes killed Little Raven's son last month. That didn't set too good with them Arapahoes."

Bottles clanked sharply as Opie shoved them

onto a shelf beneath the bar. "Hell, it don't matter which breed they is. Them Injuns want their land back and figure us whites is too busy fightin' each other to stop 'em."

Garrett's stony expression returned with a vengeance. "I wish Dick hadn't got himself mixed up in it."

Opie straightened, brushing dust off his starched white sleeves. "Yep, y'alls' got enough troubles diggin' in that accursed cemetery. Couldn't pay Timmy Jaax enough to get him to ride out there ag'in to tell ya where your pardner hied off to. Ain't a man jack in town that'd do it. Leastwise, yours truly."

I looked past him in the mirror, hardly recognizing the disheveled, schoolmarmish young woman staring back at me. From the outset, I'd expected grinding hard work, deprivations, and heartbreaking disappointments. Lord knows, I'd found plenty of each.

In my wildest imaginings I hadn't bargained on encountering bloodthirsty Indians and being caught up in a war I didn't understand and wanted no part of.

"What now, Garrett?"

He pushed away from the bar, tipping his cap at Hattiesville's pallid mayor. "Dick'll make his way to camp without us leading him by the arm.

May be there, wondering where in tarnation we're off to."

"What about the Indians? Do you think he's in any danger?"

"Naw. Those renegades were long gone before he ever got there. All that's left for us is to go home, work till daylight fails us, eat supper, find our blankets, then start over first light tomorrow."

I sighed and smiled up at him. By George, Garrett had his faults, but he surely had a way of putting things in their proper perspective.

June. Tuesday, 25th, 1861

Did not sleep any last night to speak of,
my hand pained me so bad. Bread and
butter poultice on it all night. Up before
daylight. Mosquitoes very bad. Clear
and hot.

In the two weeks since Dick's journey to the Last
Chance, he'd said little about it, which was a
revelation in itself, as were the now ever-present
sidearms tucked at the small of my partners'
backs.

To date, we'd mined earnestly, often by candlelight, eating only when too weak to swing a
pick and sleeping not nearly enough to stave
off exhaustion.

Boring deeper into the mountain's bowels created the need for shoring timbers, spaced about
twelve feet apart, in each tunnel. According to
Dick and Garrett, the same rock that defied

sledgehammer blows might crumble on our heads at any given moment.

The first trip up the ridge to fell trees for the supports, I'd smugly informed my partners that I was now hardy enough to topple a pine without breaking a sweat. In short order, I realized the stupidity of such a boast.

"Hey there, *Her*-cules—ain't you axed that saplin' yet?" Dick fairly cackled. "A beaver could gnaw off the sumbitch faster'n that."

Garrett ambled over to inspect my progress. He eyed me critically. "I've been told that ladies don't sweat, they glow." He trailed a finger across my brow, looked down, and gasped. "Jaysus, Miss Fiske. You're pert-near glowin' buckets!"

I leaned on the hickory handle as if it were a parasol's crook. "Why, mercy sakes alive, Mr. Collingsworth. Is it wise to tease a lady with an ax in her hand?"

He glanced at the tree I'd wounded and grinned like a fox, but had the good sense not to comment further.

By the next venture topland for bracing material, our spirits had lagged considerably. There'd been no capers cut, even at the supper table, for days. Tussling through games of euchre and whist before turning in required more energy than we possessed.

Dick, in particular, had become increasingly discouraged. Garrett and I gave up trying to josh him out of his bleak mood. If he spoke at all, he questioned his prospecting ability.

Maybe we should have sunk a shaft from the ridge downward.

Maybe the veined rock I'd found was a fluke, as the quartz hacked from the mine thus far didn't contain enough gold to crown a tooth.

Maybe the Swedes had brought it from somewhere else—not pried it from the canyon's pocked face.

Maybe Butcher's Gulch *was* cursed and we'd been arrogant and foolish to ignore the jinx.

Over and over, Dick'd emptied his hatful of maybes. Finishing a precious cup of weak coffee, Garrett would stare at the tunnels that ogled us like a triad of mythical cyclopes.

Slag heaps adjacent to each tunnel grew by countless shovelfuls each day. Gutting one mountain was creating three new ones in the process.

Vain as it might be, I'd gaze at Ransom's abandoned shaft, wondering how desirable he'd find me now. Without strands of twine cinching my overalls, they'd have slithered to my ankles. My belly caved like a bowl between spavined hipbones and my breasts had melted away to girlhood's mounded buds.

How ironic that I was rapidly becoming one of the boys in a way I'd never anticipated. Had I flaunted my gaunt, hollow-eyed self for another review, Opie's mirror would likely crack from fright.

But untapped bonanza or worthless borasca, we couldn't abandon The Redemption. Hope didn't cost a copper cent. It was the only essential element of human existence we could afford.

Night after night, I fell onto my bunk so bone-grinding tired that sleep eluded me. The *ching* of pick blades chipping rock rang in my ears constantly. In fact, if I had a dollar for every affliction, my pockets would have jingled merrily.

A wrinkle in my mitten or changing my grip brought fresh blisters bubbling up beside their forebears' calluses. When they ruptured, the watery liquid, sweat, and grime mixed into a slimy gumbo. The sores stung like fire when I scrubbed them to prevent infection.

Following the men's example, I'd tied a kerchief over my mouth and nose to help stanch the dust clogging the tunnel's confines. Silt coated my lashes and harried my eyes, but the cloth partly relieved one miners' misery.

Still, if I didn't think to go outside for air before the grit choked me completely, I'd stumble from the shaft wheezing and coughing up gobbets of grainy, pinkish mucus until I vomited.

Inside or out, the heat was stifling. I envied the men the ability to strip to their waists. Sadly, "Camptown Races" could be strummed on Dick's ribs protruding below the thin, graying hair wellspringing above them. There was great strength in his sinewy arms, but they appeared matchlike and frail.

In contrast, Garrett's sweat-slickened, sculpted torso gleamed like polished marble in the sunlight. I studied him with the shamelessness of an artist examining a model. Broad shoulders crested above arms treble the size of my thighs, his back tapering ever so gracefully to his waist. I wondered whether the dark, curly hair covering his barreled chest would feel downy or bristly to my touch.

Other wicked musings were better worked into submission than pondered at length, for they stirred carnal images that ladies of my station weren't supposed to have, much less contemplate.

"No color yet," we'd report in turn, needlessly, en route to the cabin. It became our battle cry, the credo of our obsession, and often, the only words uttered from sunrise to dusk.

Yesterday afternoon brought more logs tumbling into the canyon for shoring timber. Later, with Dick securing one end of a cross beam, I stood on a stump, straining to hold the other in place while Garrett nailed it to the support timber.

The stump wobbled just enough to threaten my balance. My hand slipped and caught on the projecting nail as Garrett brought the hammer down to meet it.

My knuckles took most of the impact. I jerked my hand away, unaware that the skin alongside my little finger was pinched between the nail head and the timber. I screamed in agony when it ripped free. The stump pitched out from under me.

Garrett grabbed me around the waist before my feet touched ground. I collapsed against him, shuddering with pain, afraid to look at my mangled hand.

"Get her out in the light," Dick yelled. He ran for the water bucket and dipper we kept nearby.

Garrett carried me outside and settled me gently against a boulder. The leg of his overalls was dappled with blood. My blood. Greenish yellow shimmers danced before my eyes, fading quickly to gray, then black.

I awakened lying on my side in my bunk. A couple of feet from my nose, like crows on a fence rail, Garrett and Dick perched on a bench they'd drawn over from the table. I'd seen pallbearers that looked happier than they did.

Plump as a broody hen, my hand was neatly

swathed in strips of red flannel which could only have been ripped from one of Garrett's shirts.

"How you feeling, little gal?" he asked softly. "You scared the liver outta me when you keeled over."

"My hand's throbbing like six kinds of hell, but I think I'll live."

"Prob'ly just as well you passed out when you did," Dick informed. "I kneaded it kinda rough making sure no bones was broke. Stitched your finger shut, too."

Wide-eyed, I scanned the bundle at the end of my arm as if the binding were transparent. "You sewed . . . my skin?"

A trace of the old sparkle returned to Dick's voice. "I shorely did. Watched a sawbones embroider a gash in a boy's cheekbone onc't. Didn't hardly leave no scar, neither."

Garrett knelt beside the bunk and patted my good hand. "I'm so sorry, Abigail . . ." His voice trailed off and he bowed his head.

"It was an accident, Garrett. If there's any blame placed, it lands square on my own clumsiness."

He smiled at me as if I were braver than George Washington when he crossed the Delaware. "Rest while we rustle up some grub. Hadn't noticed how scrawny you're getting until I carried you out of that tunnel."

Garrett's choice of words was far from flattering, but I marveled at both men's uplifted attitude. Had I known that pounding the whey out of my hand would have affected such a change— well, I doubted if I'd have made the sacrifice— but I welcomed their cheerfulness, nonetheless.

Unmercifully, they teased my awkward, south-pawed table manners. I matched them insult for insult. Never had a plate of Garrett's flapjacks tasted any finer.

When Dick unwrapped my hand to apply a poultice, the purpled bruise spreading from fingernails to wrist recalled the time Davy Olmstead and I painted our naked bodies with pokeberry juice. Hooting and hollering like crazed Apaches, we tore out of the cornfield to "attack" Davy's mother.

The vapors Mrs. Olmstead succumbed to resulted not from our resemblance to bloodthirsty savages, but from our unclothed condition, which puzzled me enormously. Telling her I was much more intrigued by Davy's arrowhead collection than his silly little tallywhacker had only brought on another swoon.

The fiery stings from Papa's razor strop lashing my backside had certainly diminished far more quickly than the aching throb that now kept me tossing and turning throughout the night.

As if that weren't tortuous enough, mosquitoes

seemed aware of my hampered ability to swat them. They'd hover, tickling across my face, neck, and arms before viciously impaling me to suck their fill.

Come morning, Garrett and Dick insisted I spend the day in the cabin nursing my poor wounded paw. By nightfall, that shaft number three was newly timbered and about a foot deeper than it was attests to both this woman's "goddamn mule-headed stubbornness" and what truly can be accomplished with a single-handed effort.

June. Friday, 28th, 1861

*Curtis went Home this morning. Hot
and sultry.*

I'll never know what possessed me to take my
rifle with me to the mine. Pure impulse, I
reckon, like snatching an umbrella from a hall
tree on a clear, balmy day, only to need it later
when a cloudburst rolls past.

Fumbling about during breakfast, I decided
that my bandage was too bothersome to be
borne. Verily, my hand's coloration rivaled a pea-
cock's plumes, but swinging a pick lessened its
swelling and stiffness more quickly than favoring
it had. That's what I told my partners, anyway.

Before quitting our happier home for the tunnels, we agreed that we'd accomplish more with
a midday rest and proper dinner than our habit
of chewing tallow-buttered biscuits and raw
bacon while we worked.

As for who'd do the honors, Dick pulled the short lucifer. "I'd have bet I got first crack at skillet duty," he muttered. "So what'll it be, children? T-bones and fried spuds or roast duck with that puny gravy them French folks pours over ever'thing?"

Divining fanciful menus got us all slavering before we wandered our separate ways. As I started yet another day's mindless, menial labor, visions of cherry tarts and lamb with mint sauce flashed on the scarred tunnel walls like pictures viewed throughout a stereoscope. It was enough to make me crave the inevitable flapjacks Dick was sure to fry in a few hours.

I don't know how long my growling stomach distracted me from a band of quartz girdling the duller stone like a taffeta sash.

Yanking off my kerchief, I flipped away the grit and scrutinized my find. Its veins were as delicate as cobwebs. Color. Scanty, fine, and scattered, but Lord God Almighty, it was color.

Outside, Dick called to Garrett, "I'm heading for the house and taking the water bucket with me. Give the coffee time enough to boil, then come and get it or I'll throw it out."

I took up chisel and hammer. Sweat trickled down my back and sides, my shirt plastering to me like a second skin. With careful haste, I began chipping out a brick-sized chunk and planning how I'd surprise my partners with it at dinner.

Let's see, I'll wrap the kerchief around it. Carry it at one side—no, at my waist, with my arms crossed like I'm cradling my sore hand.

I chiseled a slanting frame around the segment. If I stay a step ahead of Garrett, he'll not notice the bulge. I grinned in mischievous anticipation. That'll keep him from seeing my face, too. Papa always said I'd make a poor poker player—I can't bluff worth spit.

Wedging the tool in deeper, I pounded as hard as I dared to pry the quartz free without shattering it. Over the clang of metal on metal, I heard Dick holler.

Almost . . . almost. I was shaking so hard, I missed the chisel.

Garrett shouted something I couldn't make out.

Damn you, rock. Come on . . . just a little more. Garrett'll stomp in here lookin' for me any—

A gunshot cracked. And another. Horses—several of them—thundered into camp. I dropped my tools and dashed out the tunnel.

A blur of mounted Indians whirled and whooped near the cabin. Dick crouched in front of it, rifle shouldered and firing. Garrett's dragoon boomed from his position stock-center in the canyon. His target catapulted backward off his horse.

Flaming torches arced through the air, landing atop the cabin. A screaming brave swinging a stone-headed club heeled his horse straight at Dick. I whirled to get my Sharps from the shaft.

Hunkering behind a slag heap, I sighted a painted chest and fired. He jerked upright, then pitched from his mount.

Dick lay crumpled beside the campfire. Behind him, thick smoke boiled from the burning cabin. Garrett pivoted, slapping his pistol with his palm. Jammed?

My next two shots missed. An Indian galloped off leading Stoophy, the mule's mane bunched in his fist.

Garrett dropped to his knees and sprawled in the dirt.

I fired. A red devil's jaw exploded in a crimson splatter. Another leaped from his horse to loop a rope around Dick's ankle. The warrior took a running jump astride. I squeezed the trigger. He curled over the animal's neck and rode out, Dick's body lurching in his wake.

The others followed, one flinging another torch onto the brush arbor as he galloped past it.

I ran to help Garrett. An arrow's feathered fletching rose from a bloody wound in his side.

His cheek felt cool and clammy, but a thready pulse beat at his temple.

Terrified that the Indians would double back to finish us off, I grabbed Garrett's collar and dragged him toward the mine shafts. The toes of his boots plowed furrows in the dust, lifeless arms splaying wide, like broken wings. With every tug, blood oozed and spread wetly down his shirt.

Once inside, I drew his knife from the belted scabbard and slashed the fabric from yoke to hem. Garrett's skin puckered like lips around the arrow's shaft. It had to come out.

I probed his beefy chest. Big as he was, there wasn't much gristle between his ribs. If the arrowhead clipped a lung, he was a dead man.

I straddled his hips. "Do it. Fast, straight, and clean," I mumbled, and gripped the slender shaft at the fletching. I squinted my eyes shut and pushed—*hard*.

Garrett roared and squirmed when the arrowhead's point pierced his chest. I snapped the shaft behind it and pulled the feathered end from his back.

Streams of fresh, bright blood poured from the ugly slits. Mopping them with a scrap of his shirt only brought more burbling to the surface. I knew of only one way to stanch it.

I hastened to the cookfire. Our cabin had collapsed onto itself in a smoldering heap of charred logs. The sharp pop of a pine knot sent my heart plummeting. Before I caught my breath, an eerie, muggy calm shrouded the canyon again.

In the distance, with the leisurely grace of dancers at a cotillion, death's harbingers began waltzing across the sky. I closed my ears to their faint, jeering *ku-wee, ku-wee*.

The coffeepot was canted rakishly on a rock. One end of the pot hook had fallen into the fire during the scuffle. Using my kerchief for a potholder, I grasped the hook's cooler end to ease it from the embers. Starting away, I whirled and reached for the pot's wire handle.

As I made my way back to number two, steam and boiling coffee spewed from the spout, scalding my wrist and thigh. Heat radiated up the metal bar. I paid them no heed.

I judged Garrett's breathing to be less ragged, softer. But every tremor brought crimson beads spilling from those deep, gaping slashes.

Cradling the bar with the pot's bale, I refolded my kerchief. Couldn't risk a burn making my aim faulty. Gritting my teeth, I touched the hot iron to the entry wound.

The sickening sweet stench of seared flesh filled my nostrils. Garrett bucked and moaned;

his hands swatting weakly at the harridan causing such agony.

I held fast, praying that I was saving his life, not wrenching its last vestiges from him. The slit the arrowhead bored through his chest received the same treatment.

A gurgling groan burst from Garrett's lips. He collapsed. I tossed the cautery and kerchief aside. The edges of his torn flesh were singed and angry-looking, but the bleeding had stopped.

I knelt to peer at his flushed, slackened face. Until I noticed dark spots dappling the floor's dusty surface, I hadn't realized I was crying.

"The worst of it's over, Garrett," I whispered. "Please, just fight a little and I'll do the rest." I finger-combed strands of his sweat-stiffened hair behind his ear where they belonged.

The heaving rise and fall of his ribs was enormously comforting. I kept a vigil, arms around my bunched knees, for perhaps an hour. Garrett didn't stir, yet he didn't seem to be in distress, either.

Shadows leached from the far wall of the canyon. There was nothing more I could do for him until he regained consciousness. I crept from the tunnel.

Rounding a bend about two hundred rods from camp, I found all that remained of one of the best men I'd ever know. I snatched up rocks, hurling them wildly at the flock of carrion-eaters perched on his corpse, cackling and jostling each other greedily.

Stripped naked, Dick lay spread-eagled on his back. A wedge of bloody skull gleamed where he'd been scalped. The buzzards had already devoured his eyes and picked at his tongue and genitals.

Averting my horrified gaze from the indignities he'd suffered, I dragged him into the shade of a stately cottonwood.

"I'll not leave you to fetch a shovel. Those damned buzzards'd be after you again if I do."

I stacked a sound wall of rocks around him, jabbering all the while as if he could hear me. "I found color, Dick. Not sure there's enough to brag on, but it's gold.

"I was going to surprise you." The clap of stone meeting stone punctuated my words. "Was going to drop that pearly hunk on the table like a centerpiece. Lawsy, I can just hear you laughing—"

Looking up into that wizened, ravaged face, I fell across the cobbled mound and sobbed. "I loved you, too, you old coot. You were my friend. My partner."

Dusk was falling before I finished entombing Dick Curtis. I kept telling myself that the Lord had called him Home. That his soul was safe, unsullied, and in a better place. If only those sentiments would heal the hole in my heart left by his passing.

I turned my face to the heavens and closed my eyes. "All right, God, I'm not meaning to blaspheme You, but You've got Papa, and now You've got Dick.

"They say You don't put more on people than they can bear. Well, I'm counting on that being the true gospel. Please, don't take Garrett away from me, too."

June. Saturday, 29th, 1861

I killed a grouse on the hill. Completely
tuckered out, and thus camped, without
blankets or anything else. We roasted our
grouse and ate that without salt or bread
and dozed it off till morning, adding to
our fire every once in a while. Clear.

Garrett's mutterings and restlessness kept us both astir most of the night. I lay close by, checking for fever and dribbling cold coffee through his cracked lips. I'd never felt so helpless and ignorant in my life.

"I musta died and gone to heaven," he rasped in my ear along about daybreak. "There's an angel beside me."

I rolled over on my back, staring up at him in wonderment and relief. He was shivering and almost as white as my chemise, but that lazy grin was brighter than sunshine.

Head propped on an elbow, he leaned over me and kissed me full on the mouth, languidly and surely, as if he'd awakened me in that fashion for years.

"Wanted to do that for a long time, little gal. Figured I'd best take advantage while I can."

"Mmmm. There'll be plenty—" An odd shyness rushed through me. I averted my eyes. Things I'd prayed I'd have the chance to tell him stuck in my throat. I felt like a silly schoolgirl and was enormously annoyed at myself for it.

I touched palm to brow like a nurse absently checking her patient's condition. "Glory, you're cold as a pump handle."

Scrambling to my knees, I chafed his arm from shoulder to wrist. His wounds were purpled and raw-looking, but no scarlet flush surrounded them, indicating that infection had set in.

"That arrow drilled a couple of silver-dollar-sized holes. How bad are you hurting?"

He grunted. "Like a son of a bitch, I don't mind saying. Long as I don't do much more'n breathe, I can bear it. How'd Dick fare?"

My hesitation immediately gave Garrett the lay of the land. As I sat back on my heels, his fingers curled into fists and I'd swear his lashes grew damp.

"I buried him up the canyon beside a cottonwood. I'll take you there when you're able."

Crossing his arms over his chest, he drew his knees up. "I'm gonna miss that old sourdough."

I sensed that Garrett knew Dick's death had been neither quick nor peaceful. But until he asked, I saw no reason to give details. The remainder of Collingsworth and Company had plenty enough to fret over at the moment.

"You need something besides yesterday's rank coffee to get your strength back. Rest easy while I go see if there's anything I can salvage from the cabin."

Questioning eyes bored into mine.

"Yes, those redskinned bastards burned it to the ground. Stole Stoophy, too." I passed on a counterfeit smile and added, "Don't worry. We'll get by, regardless."

I gained my feet and started out the mine shaft.

"Abigail?" he said hesitantly. "I'm not aiming to be a bother, but could you build us a fire first? I'm chilled clear through."

My shoulders sagged. "There's nothing to light one with. Maybe if I can find some flint—"

"No need of playing squaw, gal. Got a match-safe . . ." He winced, trying to maneuver his right hand into his pocket. The clotted scab on his chest cracked. A trickle of blood wobbled from it.

"Garrett, damn it, stop ruckusing around."

Fear put a shrill edge to my voice. "I can fetch it easy enough."

"Like hell you will," he shot back through clenched teeth. "Ain't proper for a lady to go messing around in a man's pockets."

"Oh?" I circled behind him. "Well, how proper is it for a man to strip a lady buck-naked on a riverbank?"

He angled his head, squinting malevolently. "That was life or death."

I let my expression respond in kind, then slipped my hand in the gaped opening. Some trial and error was necessary before I distinguished the cartridge-shaped tin from nails, an empty money clip, and other foofaraws he carried.

"You're no lady, little gal," he growled. "Now, get that blasted fire to going, will you?"

He was sleeping again by the time the pine-needle tinder sparked scraps of shoring timber I'd gathered. Four lucifers were wasted in the process, leaving only three. There'd be no letting this fire die to ashes tonight.

As I expected, the shaft tended to trap the smoke rather than flue it outward, but as long as the wind didn't change direction, the acrid haze was tolerable.

The cabin was little more than a blackened, forlorn shell with a gap in its face, like a missing tooth, where the door had hung. Sunlight pouring out the threshold seemed to mock our loss of everything but the clothes on our backs, a few tools, and my rifle.

Raking and poking burned clumps that littered the floor with the tip of my shovel, the fusty stink of soot and bitter taste of wood ash made an unpleasant task nigh unbearable.

The flames had devoured what would burn; their heat charred or warped metal objects almost beyond recognition. I'd hoped the airtights we'd hoarded had survived, but the few tins of tomatoes I found were scorched, ruptured, and ruined.

Without disturbing Garrett, I crept into the shaft and out again, exchanging the shovel for my Sharps. The flatness of its cartridge pouch brought grim awareness: If my aim wasn't any truer than it had been yesterday, our bellies would go begging.

After I'd climbed the ridge, trembling limbs forced me to rest a goodly while. Garrett sure had a lily for a savior when he needed an oak. He was frail as a runt kitten, and I, who'd not suffered a scratch in the fracas, was faring almost as poorly.

A litany of everything we lacked, from blankets to provisions to money, droned in my head. We were lucky to be alive, but how in God's name would we survive on a few bullets, matches, and pocket lint?

Sluggish thoughts wandered across my mind until it seized upon the image of a sodbuster's widow Papa and I'd met in our travels. Cholera had taken her husband and three of her children, leaving her with two towheaded waifs, a baby due any day, and a crop of bone-dry corn rattling in the field.

I remembered the sampler she was diligently cross-stitching by candlelight. It read, "Self-pity is the lowest state to which a woman's mind can fall."

The Sharps' brass-plated butt smacked the ground. "And it's high time you got yours out of the root cellar, Miss Fiske," I muttered, pulling myself up.

Where Colorado's supposed abundance of game was spending this hot summer's day eluded me, for after an hour or better's hunt, I could attest to a decided lack of edible foodstuffs.

My anxiety at leaving Garrett alone so long was at its peak when a grouse warbled as it rustled from the brush. Before it could take wing, I swung the rifle to my shoulder, drew a bead, and fired. My tawny-feathered victim twitched a death throe as its brethren scattered to the four winds.

Grasping it by the legs, I examined my prize.

Once beheaded and gutted, I'd roll it in a ball of wet clay. After a couple of hours' roasting, we'd crack the shell like a walnut. Magically, feathers and skin would adhere to the mud jacket, leaving a succulent, albeit skimpy, feast.

"Neither of us will be loosening our belts any, Mr. Grouse, but you'll do until I go to Hattiesville tomorrow.

"That hunk of quartz I pried out has got to be worth a bag of flour and some beans. Or if worse comes to worst, with a little English behind it, it'll damn sure bust out a store window."

June. Sunday, 30th, 1861

No money. I am compelled to go it on tick.
Don't like it much, but it cannot be
helped. Clear and pleasant.

A nagging sense of failure went with me to Hattiesville. Logic said our destitution was the Cheyennes' fault and not ours, but I'd never asked for charity and never received it feeling as if I deserved it.

Alms for the poor, until now, had smacked of greed on the part of the needy too lazy to work for an honest dollar. Odd, how a catastrophe can alter one's attitude.

As sure as the sun rises in the east, there'd always be bummers extending a hand with nary a callus to be found there. But like Garrett and me, there were some folks who, if they didn't have bad luck, just wouldn't have any luck at all.

Opie had told us to call on him if we were

ever in dire straits. As the town's distinctive smells, clutter, and clatter rushed out to greet me, I hoped his offer was heartfelt.

His Honor, Mayor Joplin, proved a difficult man to find. Inquiries followed by guesses as to his location kept me weaving in and out of the commercial district's doors like a field mouse with a cat at its tail.

I caught up with my prey at his mercantile. Seated at a rolltop desk, Opie was poring over sheaves of paperwork, a garter-sleeved clerk hovering behind him.

The latter glanced at me as I leaned against the counter. Pince-nez perched midway on a narrow, sloped nose and lips screwed into a puckered scowl gave him the look of one whose drawers were cinched too short in the stride.

"May I help you?" he inquired in a tone that implied he'd rather not, if at all possible.

"I'd like to speak to Mr. Joplin, please."

"Sorry, he's—"

Opie sprang from the castored chair so heartily it almost keelhauled his clerk. "Plumb delighted to see ya, my dear." His hands fluttered a shooing gesture. "Hubert, go find ya some dust to sweep or somethin'."

The clerk's scowl was a picture of exasperation. "These accounts demand your immediate attention, sir."

"Later's soon enough. Now, scat."

Stomping toward a back room, Hubert's beady eyes held me responsible for his employer's dereliction of duty. Always the gracious winner, I smiled sweetly and bobbed my head in a ladylike adieu.

"What brings ya to town on this lovely Sabbath morn?" Opie asked. "And where's Dick and Garrett? Scaldin' their tonsils at the American?"

As straightforwardly as possible, I informed him of the events of the past couple of days.

He waggled his head mournfully, easing out a long sigh. "I won't say I told ya so, but ya damn well oughta blow that gulch to Kingdom come and let the haints have it permanent. It's plague-beset sure as cows make milk. Ain't no good gonna come to nobody there."

I unwrapped the hard-earned, rectangular chunk of quartz from my kerchief. "I wouldn't be too sure. I was crevicing this out just before the attack."

Opie gandered at it, only to peg me with doleful eyes. "Well, it's purty as a speckled pup, but them streaks is scarcer than preachers in paradise."

Earlier, Garrett had expressed the same opinion. "Even if there's a wider drift deeper in, we can't live on swordgrass and pine cones until we find it. Nobody on God's green earth ever worked harder than we have, but we're busted."

"I'm sure Opie'll give us credit enough for some supplies," I'd argued. "You'll be healed up in no time and we can get back to work."

"Listen to me, Abigail. I'm not partial to you going off alone or going begging, but we're out of choices. If we've gotta go it on tick, it's only to get us back to Denver City. Soon as I can find a job, every dollar, plus interest, will be repaid."

"I feel like a quitter."

Garrett had squeezed my hand and grinned wryly. "You're not. You've just gotta learn to admit when you're licked."

Squaring my shoulders, I held the quartz now to the mercantile's kerosene fixture, admiring how the light intensified those rusty veins.

Bullfeathers if I'd admit I was licked. Yet.

"Are you saying it's worthless, Opie?"

He raised his hands as if surrendering to a bandit. "Not a-tall. I'm sayin' what ya got there is slim pickin's."

"But is it enough to lend us a grubstake on?"

The brass bell above the door tinkled merrily. A stocky, sandy-haired man entered. He wore his brushed sack suit and pleated linen shirt as if long accustomed to tailor-made clothing.

Lowering my voice, I rushed on. "We're tapped out. I need bandages, whiskey to clean

Garrett's wounds, food, and pots to cook it in. We're good for it, I swear."

Boots thudded on the plank floor as the newcomer meandered around a turntable with a hoop of cheese atop it, pyramids of stacked airtights, sauerkraut and pickle barrels, and crates of tools.

The mercantile's owner squinted over my shoulder at the closed storeroom door, cursed, then pivoted on one heel. Gawking at the natty gent, Opie slapped his forehead with the flat of his hand. "Well, bless my soul and burn me fer a witch if Mr. Winston Parnell hisself don't sashay in here just as I was a-thinkin' about him."

Opie introduced Parnell as a representative of a mining syndicate called Aurum and Amalgamate, Limited. "A group of investors with more money than brains is keen on settin' up a hydraulic minin' operation," he explained. "Winston here's charged with findin' the mother lode and snappin' it up cheap."

Parnell laughed heartily. "A rather cursory job description, but an apt one, I suppose." He edged closer to inspect the block of ore I held. "Not a particularly heavy concentration, is it? Yet, one never knows . . ."

His eyes flicked to my attire and back to the mineral. "I've never met a lady prospector before.

May I be so bold as to ask where your mine is located, Miss Fiske?"

"Butcher's Gulch," Opie blurted.

"Is that a fact? I've heard some awfully gruesome tales about the place. Is it truly haunted?"

I shrugged. "If it is, the ghosts are a shiftless bunch. Not a one's lifted a pick, near as I can tell."

Parnell extended a hand toward the quartz. "May I?" He hefted it, then tugged a walnut-handled quizzing glass from his breast pocket.

I'll admit to fidgeting some, but Opie sidled closer and closer still until his nose almost collided with the other man's. "Whaddaya think, Winston?"

"That if Miss Fiske is at all interested in selling, I'd like to ride out to the claim for a look-see."

Hope welled inside me. I struggled to keep my expression and tone noncommittal. "My partner, Garrett Collingsworth, and I would enjoy the company."

A sly smile spread across Opie's face. "Seein' as how you're afoot, I reckon Winston could spare a horse for you, too. Ain't that right, Winston?"

"Uh, well, yes. Of course. My assayers won't be needing theirs—"

"What'd I tell ya, Abigail?" Opie howled and

clapped Parnell's shoulder. "I'll swan, women jes' simmers and stews over the triflin'est things, ya know?"

Parnell nodded slightly, though his furrowed brow indicated that like me, he had no idea what Opie was prattling about.

"When you come in," Opie continued, "I was tellin' her I owed her other partner for a wager—God rest ye, Dick Curtis. Fine man—died sudden-like a coupla days ago.

"Anyhow, I knew ol' Dick'd approve of tradin' it out in goods, but Abigail here was a-wringin' her hands and moanin' over how she'd get the stuff back to their claim."

Parnell regarded my gape-jawed stupefaction, the beaming storekeep, and back again.

"I'd be delighted to ease your distress, ma'am. I'll fetch our transportation while you two gather the supplies."

With the tip of his hat, he strode out the door. Opie started bustling about piling airtights, side-meat, tent canvas, and cooking utensils on the floor.

"Hubert!" he bellowed. "Bring a fistful o' them tow sacks. On the double!"

"Bless you, Opie Joplin," I said quietly, for my voice trembled with emotion. "We'll repay you the instant we're able, I promise."

He favored me with an ornery wink. "Now,

don't ya go to frettin' all over ag'in, woman. Git what ya need and throw in a coupla treats for the pure pleasurement of it."

Parnell's glossy black gelding and my borrowed sorrel were heavy-laden when we trotted from Hattiesville an hour later. Wisely, he'd exchanged his go-to-meeting clothes for dungarees and flannels. Before I took the lead, I noticed that he handled the reins as if he'd sat astride since boyhood.

I was profoundly curious about the man, but more concerned about Garrett's well-being. I heeled the sorrel to a canter.

On entering our camp, to my surprise, Garrett was leaning against number two's arched threshold, my Sharps laying across his thighs. Despite a hearty wave, his weakened condition was heartbreakingly evident.

The introductions were hurried and, likely, ill-mannered. I listened, but cared little for the man-talk outside. Getting a decent meal fixed and tending to Garrett's wounds was a far-sight more important. Thankfully, he'd kept the fire stoked in my absence.

Above the merry splutter of frying fatback, I caught snatches of Parnell's and Garrett's discussion.

"Me and Abigail don't have two Liberty dimes to rub together, but there's no sense in gilding lilies. Dick Curtis scraped a smidge of color down there in number one a few days—"

I startled, almost slicing a knuckle instead of the raisin loaf Opie insisted I take. Dick had found color, too, eh? Old coot hadn't seen fit to tell me. I guessed he hadn't wanted to send my hopes soaring unless more reason presented itself.

Smoke harried my eyes when I scootched around in front of the cookfire. I chose to hazard its sting rather than miss a word.

"—you saw Abigail's sample from number three. The way the bedrock's heaved, there could be a drift richer'n Croesus in number two. Except if there is, there ain't been a sign of it so far."

"I appreciate your honesty, Garrett," Parnell said. "What of that other shaft, over there? It doesn't appear to have been worked in a while."

"Hasn't. Four of us claimed The Redemption at the get-go. Down to two, now."

Garrett's clipped response told me how quickly his strength was ebbing. I filled a spanking-new tin plate with crisp bacon, sweetbread, and peaches, curled two fingers around his coffee cup's handle, and hustled out to him.

Before I'd set it beside him, he'd snatched a greasy strip and plunged it in his mouth. "Jaysus, if that don't taste fine. That's twice you've saved me, little gal."

"Oh, don't talk with your mouth full," I chided with mock sternness. "May I bring you a plate, Mr. Parnell?"

"No, thanks, but I wouldn't turn down some of that coffee if you can spare it."

While Garrett and I fell to our food like the starving beggars we were, Parnell meandered the length of the claim. Now and then, he set his cup down and jotted notes in a leather-bound book he extracted from a hip pocket.

Presently, he removed a sheaf of papers from his saddlebag and rejoined us. "I've got a gut feeling about this property. I'm prepared to make an offer for The Redemption, if you're interested."

"Might be," Garrett hedged. "Let's hear it."

"All right, I'll start by saying that not knowing how much—if enough—assayable ore it contains, only a fool'd buy it outright, and I'd like to think I'm no fool.

"If you're agreeable, I want a thirty-day contingency option on the mine. That'll give me time to bring my men in here to evaluate it."

Garrett and I traded glances. "A month's a long time to hunker on our duffs waiting, Parnell. And what's the deal contingent on?"

"If my assayers determine that the claim's

worth a two-hundred-dollar purchase price, I'll exercise the option and tender a draft in that amount payable at the Security Federal Bank in Denver City."

He smiled and added, "Fifty dollars a week's nice wages for doing nothing."

Garrett scratched at his beard. "Yeah, but only if we get it. Got expenses in the meantime, either way. Supplies and such . . ."

A great deal of self-control was needed to keep me from banging my empty plate upside my haggling partner's head. So what if Parnell had nothing to lose with an option agreement, whereas we could wind up in no better circumstances than we were? If the gamble paid off, we'd at least recover Garrett's and Papa's original investment.

"My men can start at first light tomorrow," Parnell countered. "Their assessment of other claims hasn't yet taken over a week or two. It's simply sound business practice to allow for unanticipated delays."

Garrett's eyes searched mine. His devil-take-it parley might have spoofed Winston Parnell, but it didn't cut a lick of mustard with me. Plain as the strawberry mark on his ear, Garrett was powerfully eager to sign the foolscap proffered by the syndicate representative.

"I suspicion it'll take that long before you're

trailworthy," I opined. "Might as well throw the dice and see what comes up."

The ink was left to dry while hands were shaken all around. Before he quit our company to return to Hattiesville, Parnell asked that our equipment be removed from the shafts by morning. Presumably, he meant homesteading in number two was at an end as well.

"Do you suppose our luck really could be turning?" Garrett mused aloud, almost as much to himself as to me. "Lord knows, we're due."

"Overdue, I'd warrant. Just think, that two hundred dollars'd pay our debt to Opie, buy a fine headstone for Dick's grave, and get us to Denver City—with money left."

He ran his fingers along my sample's milky surface. "It won't take a wagonload of this to get Parnell's fawnching to exercise that option, either. That's what speculating's all about. Why it's so risky.

"Doesn't matter whether it's ore or baled cotton. Once what you're after's a sure thing, the price is too dear to make a profit. Those highfalutin financiers Parnell works for are betting on the future, not the present."

Basking in the sun, hoping and supposing, we managed to polish off the entire loaf of raisin bread and a full pot of coffee.

Garrett's speech, however, was beginning to

slur. His eyelids drooped like flimsy window shades. I proceeded to dribble Forty-rod down his chest and back, which brought him howling to attention. A slug of whiskey for the inner man was gratefully and affectionately received.

After bandaging him from collarbone to belt and with a new shirt replacing the one I'd slashed to rags, he looked dog-weary, but presentable. I fashioned him a blanket pallet inside number two and helped him to it.

"You're to sleep until suppertime, and I don't mean maybe."

"Bossy female. Just wait'll I'm on my feet again. I'll get you back in line fast enough."

I pecked him on the cheek. "When hell freezes over."

He grinned far too wickedly for a man so grievously injured. "Why don't you snuggle up with me? You've had some right long days and short nights lately yourself."

"Not while there's tools to gather, a tent to pitch, and camp to make before dark. If the stink's died away, I figure we'll move nearer the cabin so I can use the old cookfire."

"Umm-hmm," formed the essence of his reply.

Glaring at the pile of burlap sacks Parnell had kindly unloaded for me, I wished I'd had the foresight to have asked him to do so closer to their final destination.

Three trips were needed to relocate all the plunder Opie had generously supplied, and I was sweating like a congressman at a revival meeting when I finished. The briny odor sent me to the ruined brush arbor in hopes that Dick's washtub had survived the flames.

Soot blackened the receptacle's sides, but as it lay rim-down in the dust, the interior was gloriously undamaged. I promised myself a soak and good scrub later, caring not a whit how many kettles of water I'd have to tote to fill it.

I thought of Dick singing and preening, getting all duded up for the dance in town. It seemed horribly unfair that he wasn't with us now, sharing our elation at Parnell's offer.

Perhaps that's why I felt like an intruder when I entered shaft number one to clear out Dick's worldly goods. If Garrett kicked and screamed about packing those picks and shovels along to Denver City, fare thee well; I'd neither abandon nor sell the old Forty-Niner's most prized possessions.

I skipped number two where Garrett slept, snoring like a bear in its winter den. The gold-speckled band in my own number three received an affectionate pat and a prayer before I left it to Providence and the discerning eyes of professional assayers.

Ransom's pitifully shallow number four contained a sledgehammer whose hickory handle showed only traces of grime and a pickax with the pointed end embedded in the wall.

"Of all the . . . *greenhorn* things to do," I spat. Pulling, then trying to wobble the pick's dangling handle didn't budge it a fraction. Cursing the day Ransom was born had no effect, either.

With a foot anchored against the wall, I took a stance as if astride a horse, gripped the handle midway between head and tail, and yanked as hard as I could.

The tool came free, along with a ham-sized chunk of bedrock. I staggered and fell, the pick handle slamming into my shoulder. Its impact and instant realization that the blade missed my throat by inches left me panting and shuddering.

Shoving it aside, my eyes rambled to the jagged gouge where it had been lodged. I didn't dare blink as I rose from the gritty floor, drawn to the site like a bee to a blooming rose.

"All that glitters isn't gold," I whispered, echoing what Dick once told me. The axiom was literal, for aurum is a dullish metal in its natural state.

I touched the lode gently as if it would vanish like pools in the desert. It was thicker than Garrett's wrist with heavy veins, like tangled, twisted strands of wire branching from it. My fingertips traced the cool, smooth treasure that men had murdered and women had sold their souls to possess.

Rage billowed inside me as fast as a prairie fire. I closed my eyes and pounded the wall with my fist.

"God*damn* this place and the hex on it. We've sold a king's ransom in gold for two . . . hundred . . . dollars."

I turned and slid bonelessly down the wall. Staring out at Butcher's Gulch, my mind was as numb as my body.

There's nothing that can be done. We can't renege on Parnell's option without tipping him off in the process. He's not a stupid man. If not for finding gold, why would we want to keep this horrid, ugly, jinxed slice of Hades? And it's futile to even hope his men could miss such a bold deposit.

Heaven above, how will I ever tell Garrett? He'll hold himself responsible, no doubt about it. If only Ransom hadn't left that blasted pick stuck in the blasted wall . . .

I tipped my head back and surveyed the breech. The slab that had concealed it rested an arm's length away. Hastening to my feet, I lifted the heavy stone and bobbled it in place. No sooner had I released it than it canted back at me.

I sprinted to the cookfire. Like a child playing

"baker's man" in a garden plot, I scooped together ashes and dirt, dribbled water atop it, and kneaded the mess into a stiff paste.

Dashing back to number four, I globbed heaping handfuls of mud into the hole and shoved the rock lid into position. Brackish gray ooze slithered from the cracks. Holding the stone with one hand, I smeared the excess with the other, tamping grit into it to better blend with its surrounds.

I took a deep breath and stepped back. Praise Jesus and all the gods in heaven, the stone held. Carrying the sledgehammer and pickax in my grimy hands, I all but staggered from the shaft.

The odds were monstraciously long that Parnell's crew wouldn't find the lode, but damned if they wouldn't have to work a mite for it.

I washed up and was preparing to stake our tent and finish making camp when I decided not to tell Garrett anything about the bonanza.

Its discovery would be anguishing enough later without agonizing over the possibility of it for days on end. Knowing him, he'd be fretting a-plenty over that option money as it was.

Garrett's the best, most trusted friend I've ever had, my partner, and all I've got left. But this is one burden I simply must carry alone.

July. Sunday, 7th, 1861

*At home all day resting, the first Sunday I
have stopped work or had rest for over
three months. Been very busy every day,
Sundays and all. Pleasant and warm.*

I hadn't had much practice keeping secrets.
Spending most of my life in a huckster's wagon,
I never had many to keep.

Papa did, and they died with him. I suppose
they were his to do with as he pleased, yet I
couldn't help believing that had he known his
last day was upon him, he'd have shared them
with me.

His reticence was born of fear that, had I been
privy to his life's darker recesses, I would have
loved him less. How sad for him to think I could
adore the man he tried to be and still turn my
back on the man he was.

It was a different kind of secret I kept from

the one I loved. Acknowledging that I did love Garrett, dearly and deeply, was revelation enough. Because of it, my silence felt doubly traitorous.

I needed desperately to talk to someone, to free the intimacies that were festering in me like embedded splinters. Only one person would understand and could be trusted with my bared soul.

Garrett was cleaning my Sharps, which didn't need it, as he'd done so daily since Winston's men arrived a week earlier. Like gathering wood, whittling, and sanding tool handles, it was busywork for a man unaccustomed to enforced leisure.

When he was flat on his back, I worried he'd not recover. His healing brought the worry that his restlessness would drive us both to addlepation.

"I'm going to take a walk," I announced to the resident gunsmithy. My rifle's brass fittings hadn't gleamed so brightly when I received it. If Parnell's men didn't complete the evaluation soon, the plating would be rubbed as thin and brittle as a codger's bones.

Garrett appeared rather startled, then said, "Give me a minute and I'll join you."

"I'd rather you didn't."

"I'll not let you wander off alone." He snapped

the rag splotched with neet's-foot oil for emphasis.

"It isn't a matter of 'let,' Garrett. I don't 'let' you do things or not do them and you're damn sure not going to govern my comings or goings."

His face took on the slack, confused look of a kicked puppy. He lowered his eyes. "That's not what I meant."

There are few things in life more infuriating than being right and knowing you've hurt another simply by standing up for yourself. I could either give in and apologize, which would turn my anger inward for being a namby-pamby, or not apologize and be thought an ogre.

As the latter better suited my mood, I muttered, "If you're lucky, the Cheyenne will carry me off," and stomped away.

The first hundred yards or so, I glanced over my shoulder expecting to find him following me and selecting which epithets I'd hurl at him. That my back trail remained empty left me wondering whether Garrett cared a whit whether savages kidnapped me or not.

Blissful solitude and striding as fast as my feet would take me gradually soothed my chronic habdabs. I also realized that was why I didn't want Garrett's company: I was exhausted from trying to appear charmingly normal when turmoil churned my innards every waking hour.

Presently, I came upon the mounded stones marking Dick's resting place. A few rocks had been dislodged, probably by predators. I replaced them, relieved that the vault I'd crafted for him was secure.

I sat down, twining my legs Indian-style. My senses drank in the sparse rill tripping over its stony path, the gentle blanket of sun warming my back, the succulent clover stem I slit with a fingernail to link it with another, then a third.

"Lawsy, Dick, it's wretched watching those men chip away at our tunnels. And cheering them on like a jockey quirting a racehorse when nobody knows the steed you've bet everything on is five furlongs behind and flagging.

"Part of me says, if Garrett knew about number four, we could share this awful anxiety. The other side argues that if squirming with the strain is grievous for me, seeing Garrett strung taut as a watch spring would be infinitely worse."

A bumblebee darted from flower to flower, frantically harvesting pollen before the giant creature plucking them from the ground, devastated the crop. I supposed the buzzing gatherer would be justified if it plunged its stinger into my greedy hand.

"I love Garrett, you know. Not only that, I like him so marvelously well. Yes, I'm sure you saw the signs long before I did. In fact, I'll wager that on occasion, you wanted to shake me 'til I rattled for making kitten eyes at Ransom. If it'd done any good, you should have.

"Lord, how I miss you, and so does Garrett. You often called us 'children,' and I guess that's the way we feel with you gone—like youngsters who aren't lost, exactly, but are terribly unsure of where they're going.

"Thanks, Dick, for listening. It helps having you to lean on. Funny, but I couldn't have talked to you this way if heaven and earth didn't separate us. Old coot, you were pretty fond of me and I'd have been afraid that admitting my weaknesses would have diminished that regard."

I rose to my feet and beheld the wispy clouds flourishing the sky. "Secrets, eh? Yes, maybe you're right. Maybe I am more my father's daughter than I realized."

The metallic clank of sledgehammers on chisels drifted out to meet me before I entered our camp proper. A harsh rasp, like coffee beans grinding in a mammoth mill, drew my attention, though I should have been accustomed to it.

I pitied the droop-eared mule yoked to the crude arrastra and concluded to sneak him his daily lick of molasses, first chance.

How boring it must be to crop in circles all day with a timber lashed to your back, dragging a boulder over chunks of rock and quartz until they're crushed fine as flour. I wouldn't have wished it on Stoophy.

Winston waved at me from his perch on the wagon's propped tailgate. Gold scales, beakers of quicksilver, and heaven knew what else littered the makeshift laboratory.

I'd learned that gold's presence wasn't a guarantee of riches. If amalgamates, such as copper and silver, were too difficult to separate from the aurum, its assayable value declined appreciably.

A vision of the wide, secret swash flashed in my mind. Surely, its nigh solid, mellow sheen promised a low percentage of amalgamates.

The peace I'd gained at Dick's grave fell away to the same badgering, unanswered questions I'd already pondered a thousand times.

What if the lode meandered north into number three or two instead of south?

How high must the assay be for Winston to justify exercising the option?

Could I withstand another hour of this inch-meal torture, much less days? Weeks?

What if the mortar holding the stone in place had dried and crumbled? That tragedy was the stuff of recurring nightmares.

Friday night instant, I'd stolen from the tent when I thought Garrett was asleep. That devil wind's moans and whistles set me a-shivering, so I ran, harum scarum for the shaft.

I'd no more than struck a match to my sole when Garrett stumbled into me. I all but spit my heart out like a tobacco plug. He couldn't conjure why I'd gone there. I couldn't explain. Later, I think he decided I was compelled to visit memories of a lost love—a bullfeathered notion, but there was no correcting it.

I chuckled at the irony of pitying that mule its mindless labor and having scant sympathy for the man who'd suffered, thus far, a week's worth of my foul moods, razor tongue, and constant criticism.

Undoubtedly, Garrett deserved more than a slurp of long sweetening for his endurance. An apology, for all past, present, and, regrettably, future transgressions was in order.

Except he was nowhere to be found. Winston's boots still dangled from the tailgate; the only occasions Garrett entered the shafts were in the representative's company.

Faint rustles wafted from the ruined cabin as I passed by. I hesitated, leery of encountering a masculine ablution that only a wife should be privy to.

Rampant curiosity quickly overwhelmed courtesy. I peeked around the door facing. The sight of Garrett's rippling broad back marred by just a palm-sized bandage thrilled me to my toes. I'd ministered to every inch of it since he'd been wounded, but ogling him from a distance was enticingly erotic.

Soap suds billowed up from his beard. He pivoted this way and that in front of a mirror fragment wedged between the logs. Light glinted from his knife's silver blade.

I clapped a hand over my mouth to stifle a gasp. He wasn't just trimming it, he was shaving his whole beard off. What had possessed him to do such a thing?

I crept to the tent and snatched up the deck of playing cards Winston had given me. The rumpled blanket made a poor table for a hand of "patience," but it was easier to cheat. Those woolly hillocks exposed the down cards if I craned my neck just right.

Hearing footsteps, I pretended rapt concentration. Garrett's shadow washed over me, but I took no obvious notice.

"I don't suppose banking three cards in a row that'd play means something besides your head's in the game, does it?"

Laughing, I scrambled the whole mess into a pile.

Garrett knelt in front of the tent flap and crooked a finger under my chin. "Little gal, do you know how long it's been since I heard you laugh?"

Like a familiar-but-unfamiliar face seen in a crowd, the one grinning at me had Garrett's high brow, angular cheekbones, and slightly crooked nose. The bowed full lips, blocky jawline, and shallow dimples were strangers to me.

"In case no one's told you lately, you're a very handsome man—with or without whiskers."

"For the record, no one's ever told me that." He blushed, and I'd swear his chest puffed a mite. "Jaysus, you're laughing, handing out compliments like stick candy—that stroll sure put you in a fine fettle."

"Garrett, I'm sorry. Very, truly, sorry for the way I've been behaving."

"Am I the cause of it?"

"Not in the least."

"Something's gnawing at you fierce. Talk to me. There's nothing the both of us can't wrestle to the ground, together."

"Getting away for a while really did—"

He shook his head. "Winston's concerned about you, too."

A warning bell tolled in my gut. The last thing I wanted to attract was Parnell's attention. "He is?"

"Hell, yes. You're spooky as a whipped cat. Clumsy and tight-mouthed whenever he comes for coffee. That isn't like you."

I averted my gaze above his flanneled shoulder. "I don't appreciate the way he stares at me. It makes me nervous."

"Hmmph. Beelzebub himself wouldn't cause

you to bat an eyelash. Nah, it's this damned waiting. I hate it with a passion and it's gotta be
worse on you."

"Wh-what makes you say that?"

He pivoted toward the mine shafts. Near as I
could tell, his eyes were locked on number four.
I could scarcely breathe. God Almighty, would
he ever answer?

"Until the last day or three, I was too puny to
care much what was going on. You've been
cooped up, fretting about me and them, the
whole time."

My secret was safe, I thought, sighing
hugely. Damn.

"Well, you may have to teach me to whittle if
I get the fidgets again, but I'll do my best to put
the kibosh to them from now on out."

"Gal, don't you know I'd tell Parnell to pack
up and take his two hundred dollars with him if
it'd make you happy?" He reared up on one knee.
"Matter of fact, I'm going to—"

"No!" I cried, tugging on his sleeve. "You can't
do that."

Please, please, don't truck with Parnell, I
pleaded mentally, *or his nose'll start quivering
like a coon hound scenting its quarry.*

"We've got a deal fair and square," I stated.
"We'll not welsh on it."

"You sure?"

"Oh, I'm absolutely sure."

With a reluctant sigh, he sat silent, his thoughts apparently miles away and in need of collecting.

Bangs and booms from across the canyon intruded on our quiet companionship. Twilight and the assayers' departure never arrived fast enough to suit me.

If any good had come from our cabin demise, it was that it forced Winston and his crew to keep their lodgings in Hattiesville. I supposed tents were for hardened prospectors, not tender-fleshed city boys.

Garrett's voice startled me from my reverie. "Reckon we've had some rough rows to hoe since we met up. Had some pretty fine ones, too."

"Yes, we have."

"I hear tell there's a for better and for worse pledge stuck in the wedding vows, somewhere."

"Uh-huh . . ."

"The way I figure it, from here to yonder, the good times'd be better and the worst downright tolerable if we stayed partners through them all."

I stared at him for a moment. "Garrett? Are you asking me to marry you?"

"I suspect I am," he drawled. "Yeah, I know, I swore to everything holy I wouldn't court any gal until I had jingle enough in my pockets. But

. . . well, Jaysus, I love you so much I just gotta hope it doesn't matter."

"I'm the one that's supposed to have the dowry, you know." I jerked a thumb toward my Sharps, leaning against a pile of provisions. "That's all there is."

He chuckled. "Always was keen for that rifle."

"Oh, I'll share it, but it stays mine."

"How about you?"

I jumped up and threw my arms around his bull neck. "I'm yours, for always, for better or for worse."

He kissed me tenderly, as if I were as fragile as a china doll. When our lips parted, we grinned at each other like mischievous children.

Thank you, Ransom, I thought, for showing me the difference between infatuation and stone-solid love.

A shout went up from number two shaft. Hank Kleiser, the assay foreman, waved his arms frantically. Winston leaped from the wagon and sprinted for the tunnel.

"By God, it appears those boys've found something in my old glory hole," Garrett exclaimed. "We may have dowries to trade yet, little gal."

I sagged against his chest, my throat constricting as if a noose throttled it. The happiest moment of my life shattered like bubbles in a strong wind.

July. Wednesday, 10th, 1861

I returned to my humble cot. Am very sick
with headache. Do not feel well.
Raining like sixty this evening.

Swaying my hand one way, then the other, I marveled at the cedar ring Garrett had just slid onto my finger. He'd spent days whittling it and sanding it smooth as a baby's cheek.

"The knob jutting up there?" he said, indicating a pear shape centered on the band. "That's supposed to be a diamond solitaire like the one I'll buy you someday."

The ring's delicate, buttery grain and faint, sweet aroma would forever remind me of the mountains I'd come to love almost as well as the man who'd crafted it.

It wouldn't withstand the decades I planned to share with Garrett, but no golden circlet or glittering jewel of any size or carat weight would ever be as precious.

"I reckon that makes us officially betrothed," he said, then paused and ducked his head like a bashful boy. "If it's all the same to you, I'd like to say our 'I do's' in Denver City with Lillith looking on. Whether The Redemption booms or busts, we'll be traveling there soon enough."

"I wouldn't have you any other way." I started to kiss him, but he raised a hand to stop me. "That's something else we've gotta talk about, little gal."

"Wha-a-at?" I asked, mildly hurt by his rejection.

His chin worked as if a cud of Bull Durham were tucked in the gums. "I'll tell you true, it ain't easy just resting beside you at night. Puts a man to thinking all manner of things."

I snorted boldly. "Don't believe for a moment you're the only one—"

"Yeah, I kinda figured that." His cheeks burned as ruddy as the hobnail lamps in Lillith's parlor. "Now, sure enough, if having relations without the nuptials sent folks straight to hell, heaven must be pert-near deserted. That's not the problem and there's no lack of wanting to, I promise. But I want to wait until you're truly my wife."

Squirming a bit, I felt like a brazen hussy for the argument poised on my lips. Yet, if he had good reason, wasn't it only fair that I knew what it was?

"I should've told you, straight up. Fact is, and I'm not trying to scare you, but there's no telling what manner of brigands and bummers we'll run into between Hattiesville and Denver City. War's got this territory in an uproar. Good sense seems to have fallen faster'n Fort Sumter."

"What's that got to do with us? I don't plan to do any sacking or pillaging to glorify either cause."

His thumb rubbed the band spanning my ring finger. "Nor do I, but if we stumble into a bad fix and something happened to me . . . I won't risk leaving you with child and without benefit of my name, Abigail. It could happen easy enough if we said 'Katy bar the door' and . . . made love like there's no tomorrow. Which is how I want to, when we do."

Never would I love Garrett Collingsworth more than I did then. Never would I be more sure of how fiercely he loved me.

Devil take him, damned Winston Parnell chose that moment to hail, "Got some Arbuckle's to spare?" and sauntered pretty as you please right into our camp.

Except from a distance, we'd seen neither hide nor hair of him since Sunday instant. Garrett had been powerfully intrigued by the hustle-bustle we'd heard, but forced himself to stay away from the mine.

As he said, The Redemption wasn't really ours

at present; an indisputable fact, but one that grated my nerves, nonetheless. The piece of foolscap we'd signed, however, did give Parnell the right to conduct his assay in private. What he wanted us to know, he'd tell us.

Garrett invited our visitor to settle himself on a stump chair. Parnell complied, then clapped his hat on a knee and ran stubby fingers through his hair.

"You look as grim as an undertaker in a ghost town, man," Garrett said, plopping down beside him.

"It's not that bad yet, but it's getting there."

Winston extended his hands for the cup I held. "Thanks, Abigail. This ought to set me to rights."

My beloved was obviously chomping to question him further, but restrained the impulse.

"I swear, if it wouldn't give my men something else to prattle about, we'd pitch tents out here for the duration," Winston grumbled. "They're blinky as barn owls from the spook stories they hear in town every night."

He waggled his head in disgust. "You've got to expect accidents. They're as much a part of prospecting as beans and flapjacks. Right?"

"Sure enough," I blurted, flexing my still-stiff knuckles.

"Well, all of a sudden, the crew's got the hoodoos as bad as darkies. Whenever somebody barks a shin or drops a sledge on his foot, they fall quiet and act real skittish. My foreman even threatened to quit Sunday when a chunk broke off and knocked Black Jack Terrill colder than a wagon tire."

"I won't deny that Opie's ghost stories had us shaking in our boots when we got here," Garrett said, chuckling.

Winston obviously saw no humor in the situation. He hardly seemed to be listening.

I picked up the coffeepot and proceeded to refill his cup just as he blustered, "Like it or not, the chicken-livers'll finish up in number three by Friday and start on number four. By God, I know there's gold—"

The pot slipped in my grasp. Scalding coffee splashed over Winston's wrist and trousers. He howled, dropped his cup, and leaped from the stump.

"Oh, Winston, I'm so sorry. Are you burned bad?"

"No worse than last time," he shot back angrily, referring to a couple of other close calls my clumsiness had caused.

"I didn't mean to. Honest, I didn't."

Garrett took the sloshing weapon from my hand. "What's the matter with you, Abigail? You're quivering like a trapped rabbit again."

"Damn it, I hate this place!" My voice rose to a piercing screech. "I hate every foot of it!"

Parnell appeared entirely too skeptical for comfort. I felt as if he could read my panicked, deceitful mind. Pure, molten fear raged through me, exploding like a fireball in my head.

"Go on, palaver till sundown if you want, but excuse me from it. I don't feel very well."

Crawling into the tent, I collapsed belly-down across the blanket. Thunder growling in the mountains resounded painfully between my temples. I lay as still as a corpse, for every movement thrust daggers into my brain.

When sleep finally came, it must have stolen me away for hours. I awoke feeling better, but strangely disoriented, as if someone had shaken me by the shoulders.

As he slumbered at my side, Garrett's even breathing was all that disturbed the rain-pattering quietude.

My eyelids popped open. I stared out the tent flap into solid blackness, instantly alert, ears pricked. Icy beads of sweat broke across my forehead.

For the first night since we staked our claim on Butcher's Gulch, no ghostly dirge was moaning through the canyon.

July. Thursday, 11th, 1861

Loafed around all morning, boys still out.
Made a pudding for dinner. Cool and
cloudy.

We whiled away the hours since sunup playing two-handed poker for matchsticks and guessing why no Aurum and Amalgamate employees had arrived for the day's labors.

It was nearly noon when we heard a horse whinny near the entrance to Butcher's Gulch. Winston rode in alone.

Garrett uttered not a word, but his face looked almost as stricken as he had when I told him of Dick's death. He caught the reins as Winston dismounted.

The syndicate representative was uncharacteristically disheveled as if he'd slept—if he had at all—in his clothes.

"Abigail, Garrett. I feel like six kinds of fool

coming here like this, but there's no getting around it."

A large, trembling hand fumbled for mine and clutched it tightly. I could feel his eyes beckoning, but kept mine on Winston. Garrett could spot a sharper at forty paces.

"My crew quit me last night," Winston announced. "Every cursed one of them. There was no talking them out of it. Believe me, I tried."

"Hattiesville's chock-full of seasoned prospectors. . . ." Garrett suggested quietly.

Winston grunted. "They're placer miners, mostly. I need men with hard-rock experience. An assayer that knows his trade. The crew I had was from California and I figure that's where I'll be going to find replacements."

He jerked open his sack coat and extracted the folded foolscap. I bowed my head to hide the elation boiling like a teakettle inside me. Though the air was cool from last night's rain, I felt feverish and clammy.

"You've been honest with me from the start and I'll return it in kind," Winston continued. "If I believed there was any way I could finish that evaluation before the option expired, I'd hold it to the last minute. But I can't and it'd be ridiculous to just let it founder until the termination date."

Garrett's husky frame sagged at the middle.

Get on with it, Parnell, I wanted to shout. Biting my lip to keep from it, I tasted blood.

"We appreciate your coming here to tell us, Parnell. Reckon this gulch was snakebit—for all of us—from the beginning."

"Then you're agreeable to ending our contract here and now?"

At Garrett's nudge, I muttered in the affirmative. He answered, "We are."

I stopped breathing for a moment when Winston stepped toward me.

"Abigail, since you brought me here and have been a most gracious, kind hostess, I think it's only fitting that you do the honors." He held the paper out to me.

Not trusting my trembling hand to a timid reach, I snatched it from him and threw it on the cookfire.

Instantly, a smudgy taint blossomed across the ivory parchment, its edges curling as if in pain. I marched to the tent and scuttled inside.

I heard Garrett explain my rudeness as aggrieved disappointment. Burying my face in the scratchy blankets, I almost expired from a fit of giggles. As the whole tent commenced rocking, I presumed the men thought I was sobbing my poor heart out.

Parnell's mount had hardly started away when Garrett squeezed in beside me. "It's all right, little gal. I know you had sky-high hopes—so did I—but I don't need a gold mine to be the richest man in the world. Not as long as I've got you beside me."

"Is he gone?" I whispered, raising from the blanket.

Garrett studied me in complete confusion. "Parnell? Yeah, he's gone—"

"I mean, *really* gone—past the opening to the gulch."

"What's it matter where Parnell's got to?"

I reared up and planted a kiss on his mouth that should've made him swoon. Then I subtly suggested he follow me from the tent by yanking at his collar. Sputtering and cursing, he rumbled from under the canvas.

I darted to the cookfire. Only a ragged, scorched corner of the contract remained. Clapping my hands, I cut a caper on the spongy ground.

Garrett stood stock-still, arms hanging limply at his sides. "Lordy, you've gone and lost your mind."

"Oh, Garrett, my darling, dumbfounded Garrett. You *are* the richest man in the world. Catch me if you can and I'll prove it."

I ran crow-straight for number four. Twisting sideward, I wasn't surprised to see Garrett's pace hardly exceed a shuffle. After all, a wise man keeps his distance from a completely deranged female.

After brushing the grit from the stone, my fingernails weren't equal to the crude mortar I'd mixed. I jogged back to Garrett and pulled his knife from the scabbard.

"Hold on!" he roared. "Goddamnit, Abigail, come back here with that."

He was right on my tail as I scampered into number four. Almost skidding into the wall, I started stabbing at stone's dark border.

"Stop it, now. Give it up." Garrett's ham-fist closed around mine. "There isn't any gold."

Cackling for all the world like Dick Curtis himself, I struggled from his grasp. "Oh, yes, there is. The most beautiful, sweetest lode you'll ever see."

I butted him away, scraping and spearing with everything I had. "I found it just an hour or two after . . . we'd signed Parnell's option. Ransom left a pick wedged in the wall. I pulled it out and . . . *Eureka!*"

Bitter grains of ash and dirt coated my mouth. I turned and spat. "Good God, Garrett, are you deaf? We've got us a fortune, for certain-sure."

"Hmmph. I ain't seen one yet."

The words were scarcely out when I pried the upper edge of the stone loose. Skittering backward, I let it crash to the floor.

Gold rippled across the aperture like burnished braid. Until that second, I was sorely afraid it'd all been a dream. That I'd find nothing but bedrock in the hole.

Garrett's chin nearly fell to his chest. He gaped, mesmerized, at the bounty that had rested not fifty feet from where Winston Parnell and his crew had been working.

"You mean you've known about this the whole time?" I heard a tinge of anger when he added, "And you didn't tell me?"

"I told Dick. . . ."

"Say *what*?"

"When I took that walk, I talked it over with Dick. Whisk me off to an asylum if you want, but telling somebody helped get me through. Don't you understand? That's why I've been so jittery and clumsy—"

"Why'd you tell a dead man and not me?"

I slipped my arms around his waist and pulled him close. "Because, believe it or not, I love you. If you'd known, you'd have gone through the same hell I have, trying not to show it."

He started to speak, but I hushed him with my fingertips. "Maybe I was wrong to keep it secret, but I honestly don't think I was. Had Parnell found the gold, I'd have at least saved you from the agony of worrying that he would."

"Yeah, but ... Jaysus, I'll bet you nigh ruptured a vital when he hoisted that paper at you."

I laughed at the memory of it. "That's why I hied off to the tent. Had he spewed any more about me being such a gracious, kind hostess, I'd of split at the seams, sure."

A throaty chuckle rumbled up his chest. "I swear, I don't know whether to kiss you or spank your ass."

"Do I get to choose?"

I didn't, but oddly enough, he picked the one I would have, anyway.

July. Friday, 19th, 1861

Bad roads, wet and muddy. Got to Denver City a little after sundown. Warm and pleasant.

"Lillith, only you could rustle up a five-course supper lamb's-tail quick," I said, leaning my sated self against the chair's spindled back.

"It's Nick Poltraine at Delmonico's who deserves all the credit. And Jezra, for his fleet-footed delivery."

Dawdling a stemmed wineglass between her fingers, she eyed the Waterford on the mantel. "We've only a few hours before the wedding, but I simply *must* know what happened after the Indians attacked."

As Garrett complied, her eyebrow arched at the mention of Winston Parnell's name. By the time he finished, she was shaking her head in amazement. "How devastating it would've been had he exercised that option. I'm afraid his bank draft wouldn't have been good enough to line a split shoe sole."

"Why? Do you know Winston?" I asked.

"I know of him. He and his Confederate cronies have made the Criterion Saloon their western rendezvous. I've been told Parnell's a proper gentleman, but the majority of speculators overrunning our fair city are vulgar clods."

Garrett smacked his lips in appreciation for the last sip of claret. "Well, if Winston's a swindler, he was the hardest working one I've ever met."

"I never called him a swindler," Lillith corrected. "After all, fraud perpetrated in the name of God, country, and the pursuit of freedom is a patriotic act. Judging by what I've heard, the Rebels' treasury can use all the patriotism it can muster and I'm sure the Union has and will commit its share of finagles, too."

"You're a born cynic, Lillith," he drawled. "If we'd needed them, there's a lawyer or three in Hattiesville and a miner's court that would've squared the matter."

"Disciples of Blackstone don't labor on tick, dear brother," she retorted. "And in a town where the Stars and Bars fly above our national banner, in whose favor do you think that court would have ruled? Yours?"

The argument was thankfully hindsighted, yet thoughts of what might have happened hardly aided my digestion. Neither did the swarm of butterflies suddenly taking wing beneath my ribs.

"Parnell and his schemes be hanged," I declared. "If I'm to be a blushing bride at midnight, I'd best start washing away the mud so you can see me do it."

Lillith's expression sobered. She laid one hand over Garrett's and the other atop mine.

"Are you two sure you want to be married in the front parlor of a sporting house?"

"Nope," Garrett grunted. "We're getting married in the front parlor of my sister's house—"

"—which just happens to be uncommonly colorful," I finished for him.

She regarded me sternly. "But you should wear white satin and lace, not—"

"Hush, now, Lillith. If superstition's making us dawdle until a minute after midnight so my intended won't see me on our wedding day, don't you dare spill the beans about my gown."

"He'll be scandalized," she warned, an impish lilt to her voice.

I gazed across the table at the object of our discussion. That unmistakably randy leer left me relatively certain he didn't care two hoots about my frock as long as buttons and hooks were at a premium.

Shrugging my shoulders, I replied, "I've scandalized Garrett since the moment we met and will likely continue to so he doesn't get bored."

"Somehow, little gal, I don't figure that'll ever be a problem."

Rising from her chair, Lillith strongly suggested that her brother find Jezra and commence getting ready for the ceremony.

Within minutes, I was blissfully neck-deep in a steaming copper tub. Frosting my skin with French milled soap lather, I realized how quickly I could become accustomed to such luxury. It would be a while before The Redemption afforded any, but when it did, I promised myself a case of those sculpted, buttery-soft bars.

Patting my skin dry, I donned a silk wrapper and hastened to a scarf-draped dressing table littered with enough potions, lotions, cremes, and cosmetics to prepare a hundred warriors for battle.

Had there been time, it would have been fun dabbling into this crystal jar and that stoppered cruet, but I'd already tarried in the bath longer than I should have.

I'd just finished blending the tiniest speck of rouge on my cheeks when Zoe, the Amazonian dove who'd promised to work miracles with my unruly mane, rapped on the door.

She stalked inside with all manner of brushes

and combs bundled in her arms. Studying my tousled hair critically, she said, "I hope you're not tender-headed."

"Didn't expect to find a rats' nest, eh?"

"Aw, now. It's the hurryin' that's the trouble, miss. No insult intended, but where I come from, jackrabbit weddings tend to come shortly before christenings."

"I assure you, there'll be only three Collingsworths in Colorado until next spring at the earliest."

Settling again in the chair, I watched as auburn snarls surrendered to her expertise. Long, tapered fingernails separated sections at the crown for braids. "If curls were money, you'd be a pauper, Miss Abigail."

"Don't I know. I once told my father that somewhere along the way, a Fiske ancestor must have tarried awhile in a tipi."

Just then, Lillith swirled into the boudoir wearing a saffron taffeta block-printed gown. Rhinestone buttons held its ruched hem, lending peeks at the lacy ecru petticoats she wore beneath it.

"You look positively regal, Lillith."

"Thank you, child," she replied, curtsying slightly. "The tailor's arrived with the mens' suits. . . ."

"I'm almost finished," Zoe said, then grinned.

"That is, if Miss Abigail will stop gandering and fidgeting."

My almost sister-in-law appeared in the mirror behind her. "I truly couldn't be happier that Garrett asked you to marry him."

"I'll do my best not to make him regret it."

Lillith smiled wistfully. "He won't, nor will you."

Her joy at our impending nuptials surely brought with it recollections of the earlier Collingsworth-Fiske union that never transpired. Perhaps, someday, she'd tell me why. Perhaps not.

Rapid footsteps tapped down the hall before the door burst open. Teresita, a petite *caliente* whose charms exceeded most men's wildest dreams, rushed in as if the El Dorado were ablaze.

"*Dios de Madre, señora,* the justice of the peace, he is loco from the whiskey."

"I was afraid that'd happen," Lillith said, groaning. "It's too much to expect a tosspot like Ben Aught to deny himself for a few hours, but he's the only official Jezra could find."

Lifting her voluminous skirts, she started toward Teresita.

"Let me handle Ben," Zoe offered, a wicked gleam twinkling from between her feathery lashes. "If pouring coffee in him doesn't do the trick, I'll splash some where it's most likely to get his attention."

"Just don't damage him overmuch. There's the ceremony to consider."

Only Lillith could have dealt, unruffled, with the hullabaloo and minor crisis that erupted every five seconds over the next hour. Of course, a saner woman would have refused the very idea of arranging a wedding on such scant notice.

The bride, admittedly, was too starry-eyed and wool-headed to be of any assistance. Naked but for a pair of kid ankle boots, I stood deaf and mute as a lamppost while Lillith gave orders, answered questions, and calmly cinched me into a corset, garters, cotton stockings, crinolines, and petticoats.

"Arms up and crossed to protect your hair," she commanded. A cool waterfall of velvet slithered over me. Careful not to muss its soft pile, I smoothed the tight, leg-of-mutton sleeves with my palms as Lillith secured the buttons in back.

"Twenty pounds ago, this was one of my favorites," she said. "But it fits as if it were made for you."

Glancing down, I was relieved that I'd filled out enough to do justice to the gown's fitted, boned bodice. In fact, from my vantage point, my bosom appeared dangerously close to escaping the bounds of the low-cut, sweetheart neckline.

Murmuring appreciative "oohs" and "aahs," Lillith showed me to the cherry-framed cheval mirror.

Lips parted in wonder, I stared at the doe-eyed, toasty-complected woman draped in yards of scarlet velvet shot with silver threads. Her burnished copper chignon and braided coronet was caught and held by garnet-studded silver combs. She was a strikingly beautiful creature. And lawsy, she was *me*.

Oh, Papa, you always told me I was pretty. If only you could see . . . A faint voice in the back of my mind promised that he could; that he was rib-busting proud of me and heartily approving of the man I'd chosen to marry.

"This is for you, too," Lillith whispered from behind me. I shivered when a delicately intertwined silver chain tickled into place. "Your father gave it to me to remember him by."

"No, Lillith. I can't—"

"Yes, you can, and will. At the time, I told Maximilian all I needed to bring him back was a quiet moment. After fifteen years, that's still all I need."

Our eyes met and held in the mirror. "Lillith, I know it's none of my affair . . ."

"And only human to be curious about your

father and me. We loved each other, Abigail, as intensely, marvelously, as a man and woman can. But Maximilian had a rambling soul and a gambler's hunger for a challenge, whereas by then I was far too independent and pampered to be happy sharing a wagon seat.

"There was also Garrett, who was away at boarding school, to consider. While your father was a brilliant man, I wanted my brother to have the formal education I lacked.

"For a time, Maximilian and I fooled ourselves into believing love was enough to change our natures. In the end, we loved each other enough to admit that trying to be something we were not would destroy us both and what we shared."

"But you never forgot him. . . ."

"Nor ever stopped loving him. I flatter myself that he retained an affection for me, as well."

Stepping back to admire her handiwork, tears glistened at the corners of Lillith's eyes. I hoped with all my heart that someday another Maximilian would come into her life to stay.

"Well, now, are you ready to dazzle my darling brother?"

"Yes, ma'am." I kissed her cheek. "Lawsy, how will we ever thank you for all you've done? My gown, scurrying to make all the arrangements—"

"Oh, name an ore cart at The Redemption

after me," she teased. "I've always wanted to be worth my weight in gold."

Downstairs in the foyer, her glossy brunette curls swayed as seductively as her hips as she preceded me into the parlor. Zoe, Teresita, and three other Cyprians I hadn't met formally, perched on chairs and on the horsehair settee.

Awaiting my entrance, I kneaded a small leather pouch, my fingers caressing the contours of a pebble from Dick's grave, Garrett's cedar ring, the arrowhead that could have denied us this day, and a dab of gold from our mine. With Papa's silver chain encircling my neck, everyone I loved, in some way or another, was present and accounted for.

Lillith moved aside. I glimpsed a bald, ruddy-faced gnome in a rusty shadbelly and crooked string tie clutching a table's edge as if primed for an earthquake. Justice Aught, I presumed. Nearly as I could tell, his rumpled trousers hadn't received the dousing Gertrude had threatened.

Jezra's black leather high-lows creaked like crickets when he hurried in to provide me escort. I reckoned he'd grow into that spanking-new boiled shirt, frock coat, and long pants before year's end.

Garrett turned as I crossed the parlor's threshold. Without question, my beloved was born to wear a satin-lapeled swallowtail and trousers with satin stripes at the seams.

His hair had been trimmed to fall in waves to his shoulders, his mustache clipped and waxed to perfect points.

Never taking his eyes from mine, he reached for my hand.

I took it, and my rightful place, neither a step in front or one behind, but beside him, where I belonged.

Finale

Abigail gently closed the diary and hugged it to her breast. Memories of the forty years that had elapsed since its final entry whisked through her mind like autumn leaves in a dervish:

Her and Garrett's founding of Collingsworth Consolidated Mining and Minerals, and how quickly they'd become wholly responsible for hundreds of workers' daily bread.

In its heyday, The Redemption and its sister mines yielded over fifteen thousand dollars per week in gold, silver, and copper; a fortune, to be sure.

Yet, many a night, its owners lay in bed, fingers laced tightly, fretting over labor strikes; mourning faceless miners who'd been buried alive when tunnels inevitably collapsed; worrying about unexpected market fluctuations, expenditures that could drain their working capital—a thousand and one costly, emotional tolls their employees couldn't fathom, much less appreciate.

The birth of Constance Lillith and, two years later, Lucille Curtis—adorable strawberry-blond cherubs Garrett had relentlessly spoiled and Abigail loved fiercely, but ceased to understand about the time their hems reached sidewalk-brushing length.

Lillith's marriage to transplanted Englishman Lord Walter Noble. How well Lady Lillith Noble fit her new name and the role of a northern California cattle baron's wife. And how quickly San Francisco's other Russian Hill residents forgot the gracious lady's ignoble past.

Garrett's death, nine years ago. A massive stroke, Dr. Adams had said. The insurance company's paperwork listed Abigail as his "survivor." It seemed oddly appropriate, for she had survived the raw, gaping chasm left by his passing, but never recovered from it.

Constance's son, Fiske Purdue, who presumed himself heir to the Collingsworth throne. Trouble was, Fiske could not, despite a Harvard degree, manage his way out of a burlap sack.

Tall, fair-haired, handsome, and totally lacking in practical skills, her undeniably charming grandson had always reminded Abigail of someone, but she could not quite put her finger on whom.

It was Lucille's daughter, the penny-bright, vivacious Abby, who positively glittered with ambition. She was taking Colorado's School of Mines and Metallurgy by storm and would, when her father David Honeywell and uncle Robert Purdue retired, ascend to the presidency of Collingsworth Consolidated.

Abigail chuckled wickedly, thinking of yesterday's board of directors' meeting when she'd casually dropped that hereditary bombshell. Why, she hadn't seen such shocked, stricken faces since 1892 when she'd been invited to speak— as one of the city's last breathing museum pieces—to the snooty Daughters of the Denver Pioneers Club.

Looking out from the lectern at the sea of fur-bedraped, jewel-encrusted matrons, she'd launched into a vivid description of being married in a whorehouse by an intoxicated official, with the establishment's madam as her maid of honor and a twelve-year-old colored boy attending Garrett as best man.

While Abigail emphasized that it was truly a historic event, which, to the best of her knowledge, had never been duplicated, both Constance and Lucille fainted dead away in their front row seats and had to be revived with liberal doses of smelling salts.

"Oh, my darling daughters," Abigail mused

aloud. "Will you ever grow tired of judging your worth by what those pickle-pussed ninnies think of you?

"There's so much more to life than worrying whether your silver pattern's all the rage or if your foyer's flower arrangements are 'simply precious' enough to make an enviable first impression."

Shaking her head, she reached into the trunk and drew out a small leather pouch. There was no need challenging her gnarled fingers to loosen its drawstrings. Other than the addition of the silver chain, it held the same keepsakes it had on her wedding day.

"Lawsy, what a glorious reunion we're about to have up yonder, dear ones."

Her heart skipped a beat, then another. A wave of dizziness assailed her.

She eased from the chair and onto the dusty plank floor. "Damned if I'll meet Saint Peter with a pump knot on my forehead."

Everything was in readiness. A few hours ago, the Christian Foundation for the Poor's drayman had loaded carton after carton of donated clothing—every dress Abigail owned, save one.

A messenger had picked up a memo containing detailed instructions as to how her funeral should be conducted for prompt delivery to her attorney. Since she didn't completely trust the dandified little weasel, a copy was sent to her devoted granddaughter, Abby Honeywell.

Before climbing up to the attic, Abigail had carefully brushed the dust and wrinkles from the shot-silver, scarlet gown her daughters so vehemently despised.

All that mattered was that Garrett had loved it, just as he'd loved the bride who'd worn it.

"I'm not meaning to blaspheme you, Lord," she gasped, her chest constricting painfully. "But, so help me . . . if Connie and Lucy lay me out in dratted . . . black . . . widow's weeds, I swear . . . I'll come back . . . and haunt 'em."

Abigail's eyes fluttered and closed. The diary skidded into her lap as she slumped against the trunk.

Dressed in a black swallowtail and trousers, silhouetted by shimmering, golden light, Garrett smiled at her, and reached out his hand.

THE ROCKY MOUNTAIN NEWS
Denver, Colorado
August 23, 1901

A private funeral service for Missus Abigail Fiske Collingsworth, business partner and widow of Collingsworth Consolidated Mining & Minerals' magnate Garrett Collingsworth, was held at two o'clock yesterday afternoon at the Church of the Holy Redeemer.

According to her wishes, Missus Collingsworth went to the Lord wearing an antique velvet gown and clasping a bouquet of Rocky Mountain columbines, a drawstring reticule, and a small leather-bound journal.

In the family plot on the Collingsworth estate, near the graves of her father, Maximilian Roswell Tremain Fiske, sister-in-law Lady Lillith Noble and cherished friend, Dick Curtis, Missus Collingsworth was laid to eternal rest beside her beloved husband.

Author's Note

While Abigail Fiske is entirely a figment of my imagination, her name was derived from Colorado prospector Abijah Fisk Gore, whose journal entries open each chapter of this novel.

A decade has passed since I held Mr. Gore's small, leather-bound diary in my hands, marveling at the clarity of his penciled notations which had been written, undoubtedly by candle or lantern light, over a hundred and twenty years earlier.

It is in honor and memory of him that I have left the entries in *Redemption Trail* as authentic reproductions of the originals, including Gore's description of each day's weather conditions.

Because references to "Dick" and "Curtis" cropped up repeatedly in Gore's journal, I took the liberty of combining them as the character name for my irascibly lovable Forty-Niner.

"Stoophy" the mule was prompted by a similar

mention—or, rather, a humorous misunderstanding. Due to Gore's occasional spelling lapses, unique punctuation, and a tendency to use the antiquated *fs* in words containing a double *s*, I repeatedly misread that entry as: *Started from camp early, had a cat's-afs. Stoophy, a mule fell off the bank into the Blue River. . . .*

When it finally dawned on me that Gore had simply cobbled the spelling and spacing of "catastrophe" rather than calling the calamity a "cats-ass" and the mule involved "Stoophy," I was so enamored by the animal's accidental moniker that I saw no good reason to change it.

Phil the Cannibal and Father Dyer, as disparate in personality as two men could be, were as much a part of Colorado Territory's history as Zebulon Pike and in their day, equally as famous—or infamous, in the former's case.

In addition to Father Dyer's incredible shoe-leather ministry, he also delivered mail to his widely scattered flock and acted as a gold dust courier.

As for Phil the Cannibal, it's hardly surprising that his body was found quite riddled by "unnatural causes."

The novel's place name "Butcher's Gulch" was inspired by Gore's haunting description of "Dead Man's Gulch" as reproduced in chapter twelve, but its actual locale conflicted with where I needed Collingsworth and Company to find their treasure trove.

Unfortunately, the results of Abijah Fisk Gore's eighteen-month fortune hunt could have been measured in ounces, not tons. According to his journal's final entry dated July, Friday 12, 1861: *The Company splitt this Morning, some going Home & some to the new Gulch, upon examination our grub was found low down so we concluded to go Home, too.*

Despite the entry's melancholy tone, Gore may have been down, but was certainly not out. Upon his arrival in Saint Louis, he enlisted in the Union's 2nd Iowa Infantry. Although wounded in the battle of Fort Donelson, Gore re-upped in 1863 and was among the legion of 110,000 General Sherman marched to the sea and back again.

Ever the wanderer, Gore later managed a general mercantile in Joplin, Missouri, and in 1889 became an impatient "Sooner" waiting eagerly for the shotgun-started Oklahoma Land Rush.

Abijah Fisk Gore lived to the ripe old age of sixty-eight, but despite the numerous avocations he pursued, he always, proudly, referred to himself as a gold miner.

I am forever indebted to Vernon Gage for allowing me to peruse and photocopy Abijah Fisk

Gore's priceless eyewitness record of a Colorado gold mining adventure.

If only all caretakers of historic documentation were so generous with their treasures, we contemporary snoops might glean an even sharper perspective of the past, its people, and their trials, tribulations, joys, heartbreaks, and amazing accomplishments.

WE INVITE YOU
TO PREVIEW
SUZANN LEDBETTER'S
NEXT THRILLING NOVEL
OF THE WEST,

FRENCH'S FOLLY

COMING THIS FALL
FROM SIGNET

Jenna Wade French stretched on tiptoes to take her husband's photograph from the whipsawed mantel. She peered at Guthrie's goateed countenance, how the flash of phosphorous had blanched his blue eyes to a ghostly pewter.

Her fingertips traced his features, boyish even at twenty-six. A face too innocent to inspire distrust had been key to Guthrie's dubious success.

Laying the oval frame on the cabin floor, she planted a heel squarely at the bridge of his nose. The glass snapped like a pistol shot. Spiderweb cracks darted at myriad angles.

"You were a scoundrel, head to heels, Guthrie

French," she said. "I'm sorry you're dead, but not a jot sorry you're gone."

She gripped the hearth brush in one hand and ash shovel in the other. Kneeling to clear away the jagged shards and glittery bits, she recalled their whirlwind courtship.

"It's a whole new world I'm bound for, Jenna," he'd proclaimed a few days after they'd met. His horse had thrown a shoe, and he'd happened upon the Wade farm hoping for a replacement. "For all the newspapers and books boasting of the West's wide-open spaces, can you imagine glaciers reaching their icy noses to the sky? Millions of acres of primeval forests too glorious for artists to capture in oil?

"Come with me to Canada, darling. We'll be the Adam and Eve of the wilderness."

It had all sounded so romantic to an eighteen-year-old farm girl destined to marry a local boy and raise chickens, hogs, crops, and children on a plat of stark, midwestern prairie.

On August 9, 1871, no sooner than a circuit-riding preacher declared them man and wife, they'd headed northwest on horseback. Their union was consummated on a grimy blanket; the act witnessed by the pair of ear-twitching mares tethered nearby.

Guthrie had rolled off her and onto his side. Within minutes his ghastly snores competed with coyotes yipping at the silver moon. Jenna lay awake a long time, wondering what had inspired all those songwriters' and poets' passionately romantic notions.

"Adam and Eve?" She chuckled mirthlessly, edging the shovel's lips over a crack in the floorboards. "For three miserable years we scrapped like Cain and Abel. And Guthrie's fascination with Canada lasted only until snow swirled to ten-feet drifts and chilblains numbed our faces and feet."

Despite the murderous weather, her affection for the land had evolved into an abiding quality. There was more than simply twenty-two hundred miles separating the rugged Cassiar District from Hay Springs, Nebraska.

British Columbia's savagely beautiful terrain was as awe-inspiring as it was treacherous. Mere words couldn't describe how dawn bathed cloud-derbied mountain peaks and glaciers in salmon pink light, deepening to majestic blues and purples. She'd seen river canyons so steep their rims seemed to graze the sky and vast, wildflowered meadows that magically emerged from beneath winter's heavy blanket of snow.

Glass tinkled merrily as Jenna dumped it in the ash bin. "We could have been happy here, if you'd only loved me back. Needed me for something besides a shill for your schemes, a bed warmer, and—"

Knuckles rapped sharply on the cabin door. After smoothing her hair from her forehead and the wrinkles from her cheap wool skirt, Jenna opened it just enough to recognize "Cayuse" Mike Duncan's wind-burned cheeks appled above his sandy beard.

"May I come in, Missus French? It's a sad day to be sure and a blustery one here on the stoop."

Good manners overcame the clenching sensation in her belly. She motioned him inside, then shut the door against the frigid wind, leaving the thong latch dangling.

The region's most successful entrepreneur smiled kindly at her while he removed his mittens, malmot hat, and turka. He stood only an inch or two taller than her five feet five and likely outweighed her by no more than a stone, but his presence filled the chilly, dark room.

He took stock of the narrow bunk draped by a tattered quilt, the upended barrel that served as a table with two crates for chairs. A whomper-jawed oak safe near the fireplace held tin plates, mugs, a fork, two spoons, a carving knife, a scoured iron skillet, and a dented bucket.

If it's high tea you're expecting, there's not

enough food in that cupboard for mice to trouble themselves, Jenna mused. Especially for one whose breath smells of fruit brandy and two-bit cigars.

"You've made a cozy nest from this breezy old shack," he said, rubbing his palms together.

"What do you want, Mr. Duncan?"

His slate eyes widened innocently. "To offer condolence at your husband's passing, of course. Why else would I be here?"

She hugged her arms to her chest. "Let's see, there's rent money overdue, Guthrie's gambling debts to collect . . ."

"Do you think me so flint-hearted as that?" He settled cautiously on a crate. "It's hardly my fault that your husband preferred fleecing others out of their hard-earned cash to working for an honest dollar."

Ah, and the pot does call the kettle black, she sneered silently. Her uninvited visitor and his henchmen plundered the Cassiar's riches as ruthlessly as pirates once controlled the seas.

Aloud, she replied, "Guthrie left little more than a gold-plated watch and a pair of sterling cufflinks, but you'll get what's owed you. Somehow."

Duncan flicked a spot of mud from his

custom-tailored, pinstripe trousers. The dapper scoundrel always wore suits, silk ties and boiled shirts more appropriate to a State-side banker.

"I take it, Guthrie didn't tell you of his latest project?"

An ominous shiver ricked Jenna's spine. She'd never been able to decide which was worse: knowing what skullduggery her husband was perpetrating and on whom or remaining ignorant until his outraged victims accosted her on the street.

A chuckle rumbled from Duncan's throat. "You're far too pretty to wear such a grim expression, my dear. It's good news I've brought you, not bad."

"Oh? And what might that be?"

"Several months ago, Guthrie borrowed seven hundred dollars to buy a herd of cattle and have it shipped by steamer to Glenora—"

"Wha-at!" Her heart plummeted to her boot tops.

Duncan raised a manicured hand. "Hear me out, Missus French. The animals are due to arrive tomorrow morning. I'm prepared to buy them for three thousand dollars, minus the amount your husband already owed."

Jenna mentally calculated the difference.

"Ye gods, that leaves twenty-three hundred dollars."

"Actually, twenty-one," he corrected. "Lady luck abandoned your beloved a while back during a hotly contested hand of poker. I covered his losses."

Jenna winced, remembering all too vividly Guthrie lurching into the cabin, raving at being cheated by a card sharp named Quincy Trent. Questioning why he'd challenged a professional in the first place was answered with the back of his hand.

Duncan rose to his feet. "There'll be a bank draft made out to you at the River Queen by noon tomorrow. That is, if you don't mind being seen entering a gaming house."

Jenna hesitated, a warning rattling in her mind. "Might I have a little time to consider your offer?"

Duncan's eyes narrowed to a feral squint. Hastily she added, "Not that it isn't generous. But so much has happened the last few days, what with Guthrie's passing and all, why, I simply can't think straight."

He squeezed her forearm gently. "Though I realize no amount of money can relieve your grief, such a sum will ease your circumstances. It's the future you must think of, Missus French."

Don't try to con a con man's widow, Mr. Duncan, Jenna thought, lowering her gaze demurely. If Guthrie taught me anything, it's that deals that seem too good to be true always are.

"I will, sir," she assured. "I can promise you that."

WHISPERS OF THE RIVER
BY TOM HRON

They came from an Old West no longer wild and free—lured by tales of a fabulous gold strike in Alaska. They found a land of majestic beauty, but one more brutal than hell. Some found wealth beyond their wildest dreams, but most suffered death and despair. With this rush of brawling, lusting, striving humanity, walked Eli Bonnet, a legendary lawman who dealt out justice with his gun ... and Hannah Twigg, a woman who dared death for love and everything for freedom. A magnificent saga filled with all the pain and glory of the Yukon's golden days....

from SIGNET

Prices slightly higher in Canada.   (0-451-18780-6—$5.99)

FALCONER'S LAW
BY JASON MANNING

The year is 1837. The fur harvest that bred a generation of dauntless, daring mountain men is growing smaller. The only way for them to survive is the way westward, across the cruelest desert in the West, over the savage mountains, through hostile Indian territory, to a California of wealth, women, wine, and ruthless Mexican authorities.

Only one man can meet that brutal challenge—His name is Hugh Falconer—and his law is that of survival. . . .

from SIGNET

THE DAWN OF FURY
BY RALPH COMPTON

Nathan Stone had experienced the horror of Civil War battlefields. But the worst lay ahead. When he returned to Virginia, to the ruins of what had been his home, his father had been butchered and his mother and sister stripped, ravished, and slain. The seven renegades who had done it had ridden away into the West. Half-starved and afoot, Nathan Stone took their trail. Nathan Stone's deadly oath—blood for blood—would cost him seven long years, as he rode the lawless trails of an untamed frontier. His skill with a Colt would match him equally with the likes of the James and Youngers, Wild Bill Hickok, John Wesley Hardin, and Ben Thompson. Nathan Stone became the greatest gunfighter of them all, shooting his way along the most relentless vengeance trail a man ever rode to the savage end ... and this is how it all began.

from **SIGNET**

Prices slightly higher in Canada.   (0-451-18631-1—$5.50)

DESERT HAWKS
BY FRANK BURLESON

The year was 1846—and the great American Southwest was the prize in an epic conflict. The U.S. Army and the army of Mexico met in a battle that would shape the course of history, while the legendary Apache warrior chief Mangus Coloradas looked on, determined to defend his ancestral lands and age-old tribal traditions against either of the invaders or both. On this bloody battlefield young Lieutenant Nathanial Barrington faced his first great test of manhood ... as he began a career that would take him to the heart of the conflict sweeping over the West from Texas to New Mexico ... and plunge him into passion that would force him to choose between two very different frontier beauties. This enthralling first novel of *The Apache Wars* trilogy captures the drama and real history of a struggle in which no side wanted to surrender ... in a series alive with all the excitement, adventure of brave men and women—white and Native American—who decided the future of America.

from **SIGNET**

Prices slightly higher in Canada.   (0-451-18089-5—$4.50)

COYOTE RUN
BY DON BENDELL

On one side stood the legendary Chief of Scouts, Chris Colt, with his hair-trigger tempered, half brother Joshua, and the proud young Indian brave, Man Killer. On the other side was a mining company that would do anything and kill anyone to take over Coyote Run, the ranch that the Colts had carved out of the Sangre Cristo Mountains, with their sweat and their blood. Their battle would flame amid the thunder of a cattle drive, the tumult of a dramatic courtroom trial, the howling of a lynch mob, and a struggle for an entire town. And as the savagery mounted, the stakes rose higher and higher, and every weapon from gun and knife to a brave lawyer's eloquent tongue and the strength and spirit of two beautiful women came into powerful play.

from SIGNET